**"You were made for moonlight,"
he whispered.**

"Or was moonlight made for you?"

The last vestiges of rational thought evaporated. As Ethan ran his hands through the shimmering tresses of her hair, she could only think of wanting him, wanting him with a desire that was nearly painful.

"I came out here to get some air," she said, weak beneath the smoldering beams of his eyes, "but I still can't seem to catch my breath. Maybe we'd better go back in."

"They're playing our song again . . . and I believe we're alone, this time. Miss Farr?"

Wordlessly, she fell into the circle of his strong arms.

Dear Reader:

Spring is just around the corner! And we've got six new SECOND CHANCE AT LOVE romances to keep you cozy until it arrives. So sit back, put your feet up, and enjoy . . .

You've also got a lot to look forward to in the months ahead—delightful romances from exciting new writers, as well as fabulous stories from your tried-and-true favorites. You know you can rely on SECOND CHANCE AT LOVE to provide the kind of satisfying romantic entertainment you expect.

We continue to receive and enjoy your letters—so please keep them coming! Remember: Your thoughts and feelings about SECOND CHANCE AT LOVE books are what enable us to publish the kind of romances you not only enjoy reading once, but also keep in a special place and read again and again.

Warm wishes for a beautiful spring,

Ellen Edwards

Ellen Edwards
SECOND CHANCE AT LOVE
The Berkley Publishing Group
200 Madison Avenue
New York, N.Y. 10016

STARFIRE

LEE WILLIAMS

A SECOND CHANCE AT LOVE
BOOK

Second Chance at Love books are published by
The Berkley Publishing Group
200 Madison Avenue, New York, NY 10016

to
Susan—
who helped to
make it real

STARFIRE

Chapter

1

AMANDA FARR HAD come into the Glen at the crack of dawn to be alone, and another human being was the last thing she wanted to see. So when she first noticed the man sitting on the wooden bridge that crossed the river up ahead, she froze in mid-stride. The golden spruce branches arching above her head rustled in the wind. Her long, raven-black hair flew about her face, and she shook the tresses from her bright blue eyes, her lips pursed in a pout of vexation. Out of two square miles of gloriously autumnal woods, why had someone chosen her favorite spot to settle down in? And why in her favorite hour, the hour when students from Deermount College and the townspeople of Silver Falls were usually still asleep?

The forest preserve wasn't hers, of course. But over the years she'd claimed this place where the Silver River ran deepest as her own. She'd been looking forward to sitting on the little bridge in solitude for days now. She was almost at the end of a particularly busy teaching week, and watching the powerful rush of water underneath would have been the perfect way to catch her breath and clear her mind.

But now a stranger had taken her spot. He was seated, legs dangling over the side of the bridge, an open notebook in his hand. His head was bent, his pencil poised. Amanda scrutinized him from fifty feet away. His auburn hair was unkempt, his tight jeans faded, and the tips of

1

his leather boots muddy. A tuft of burly chest hair peeked out from the open collar of his flannel shirt. The seriousness with which he regarded his notebook seemed at odds with his farmhand style of dress. He wasn't a student, she assumed; he looked older than that, and too rugged. Nor did she recognize him as a native of the small Ohio town. At another time or place Amanda might have found him extremely attractive. But at the moment, he was an obstructive nuisance.

She knew she couldn't just ask him to leave, but she was in no mood to make a new acquaintance. She'd barely been out of bed an hour, and mornings weren't her most sociable time. As she felt the wind ruffle the ripped seat of her old corduroys, Amanda was reminded that she wasn't dressed to socialize, either. She decided to return in the direction from which she'd come and avoid the man altogether.

He hadn't sensed her presence yet. He seemed lost in thought. Still facing him, Amanda took one tentative step back, glad she was wearing her sneakers. With her green ski sweater and black cords, she could almost blend in with the scenery. Perhaps if she were quiet enough...

The tiny crunch of leaves beneath her was obscured by the sound of the river. She took another step backward, watching the man. He still hadn't looked up. Stealthily, she continued moving back, one step at a time.

Then her foot came down on an unforeseen tree root, and she was thrown completely off balance, perilously close to the water's edge. In the next fleeting instant she struggled to regain her footing, failed, and then all thought was wrenched from her spinning head as she fell—sky, earth, and her own limbs a flurry of whizzing color in her face.

She hit the water. Her ankle smacked against a rock

as she went under. Desperately she wrenched her body upward, broke the surface, spluttering and gasping, and felt herself pulled backward in the river's icy clutch. Water assaulted her eyes and nose. The weight of her soaked clothing slowed her frantic kicks against the current. Foundering in panic, she could barely believe what was happening.

Suddenly, as she continued to struggle, she felt the viselike grip of strong fingers on her wrist, felt, but couldn't see, a steady arm behind her back. A force more powerful than the river was propelling her sideways. Her body bent to it of its own accord. She stopped struggling. A firm pressure at the back of her neck compelled her to face up, to gulp in air. A solid mass of weighty muscle dragged her from the freezing depths and hoisted her above the surface.

Then she was in the air, heaving and panting in the sturdy arms of a man, clinging to his brawny chest. She went limp as he carried her, her head falling back on his shoulder, her eyes closing in exhaustion. She was dimly conscious of being lowered to the ground. Then her consciousness faded for a moment. She felt her arms lifted as though they were someone else's, was fuzzily aware of her sweater being pulled up over her face and off. Deft fingers undid the top buttons of her shirt, then gently massaged her neck, feeling for her pulse.

Her eyes blinked open and tried to focus. When she looked up, she was gazing into the dark velvet depths of the man's eyes. They held hers in a moment of pure magnetic attraction. Amanda gasped. And then the moment was gone.

"Breathe," said the man. "Just breathe."

She inhaled, a slow, shuddering breath.

"That's better," he said. "Keep it up."

His voice was deep and caressing. She heard oakwood in it, and a stream's silky rustle. There was an easiness, a seductive lilt in his tone that evaporated every thought in her head. Lying on the damp ground, she was unable to do more than breathe slowly and try not to melt beneath those eyes as he leaned over her.

Instead she looked at hard lines that etched a ruggedness into his smooth, tanned skin. There were smaller, soft smile lines around his taut, sensual mouth. The velvet softness of the amazing eyes diffused the tough, craggy quality of his firm jaw and high cheekbones. His face, she reflected, had both a trace of boyish openness and a hint of seasoned maturity. Close up, he was far better looking than she had imagined—he was devastating, in fact. He was perhaps the best-looking man she had ever seen.

His expression was disconcerting. He was watching her take his measure with a good-humored, almost arrogant air. He looked like he was . . . reading her.

"I think you'll live," he said, stroking her eyebrow with a single fingertip. His touch was delicate, but its effect was deliciously soothing. "How do you feel?"

"Waterlogged," she murmured, almost hypnotized by the husky reverberations of his voice. He smiled. Amanda found herself smiling back, though she hadn't meant to.

His fingertip, now tracing a light trail along her cheek, was sending shivers down her spine. And even as she became aware of the frigid wetness that chilled her, she felt the stirrings of a strange, sensual warmth welling up in the very core of her being. It occurred to Amanda that this man had a power that bordered on dangerous.

"Not azure, not cobalt . . ." he muttered, his eyes probing hers with a steady, riveting gaze.

She blinked, confused.

". . . not powder, but . . . *sky*-blue," he pronounced triumphantly. "That's the one fitting word for those eyes of yours: sky-blue."

The sensations his own eyes were provoking in her were a little dizzying. Though she knew she was stretched out on the ground before a total stranger in the midst of a secluded woods, she couldn't bring herself to move. Gently, he lifted her chin with his hand.

"Are you a member of some kind of Polar Bear Club?" he asked.

The hint of condescension she thought she detected behind his mock-innocent query brought Amanda to her senses. She removed his hand from her face and strained to sit upright.

"Yes, that's right," she said. "I was in such a hurry to get into the water, I forgot my bathing suit." She'd succeeded in sitting up, but removing herself from his reach seemed too difficult just now.

"And your bathing cap," he added, eyes twinkling. He gave her hair's length an admiring glance. "Say," he went on, forcing down a grin, "what do you call that odd dive you did? Back belly-flop? Triple twist—"

But before he could finish the list, Amanda was struggling to get up, flushed with embarrassment. He'd seen her fall, then. It took every ounce of strength in her weakened body, but she managed to scramble unsteadily to her feet. In doing so, quite unwittingly, she shoved him, knocking him off balance from his crouching position, and he fell back to the ground.

With smooth, athletic grace he was up again almost instantly and stood to face her, an amused expression on his face. She trembled before him, hugging her arms to her wet body as his eyes roved over her, stroking her from shoulder to toe in a single appreciative glance.

Amanda felt as if his gaze had melted her clothes off. She was suddenly acutely aware that she was braless, the clinging wet shirt no doubt vividly outlining the curve of her breasts.

"You're certainly strong," he said, smiling. "Maybe I should have left you in there to fend for yourself." He was looking at the palm of his hand. She saw a smear of blood.

"Good Lord!" she exclaimed, immediately contrite. "What did I—?"

He waved her back as she hovered closer to him and inspected the ground. "Just an inopportune rock," he said, kicking it out of the way. "You're the one with the injury. Let's see if it's serious."

She followed his glance to her left foot. The top of her white sneaker was stained with red. She hadn't had time to register the throbbing of her ankle, but she felt it now.

He knelt in front of her. Amanda tentatively rested a hand on his broad back to steady herself as he lifted the injured foot. She tried to keep her eyes off the supple musculature rippling through his wet shirt. The man pushed the cuff of her corduroys up, inspecting the little half-moon of blood above her ankle. She felt a dull stinging as he gently pressed the skin around it, but she could see the cut wasn't deep.

"You're lucky. It's just a nick. Does it hurt?"

"No," she told him, more concerned with the warmth that emanated from his hand on her thigh. He rose and noticed her chattering teeth.

"Your lips are turning blue," he said. "Wait here a second."

He sprinted down the trail to the bridge. A bit bewildered, still feeling the phantom imprint of his body against hers, Amanda watched her rescuer retrieve his notebook and jacket. Then he was back, placing the jacket across her trembling shoulders. She chanced a look in his eyes, and he held her look.

Time seemed briefly suspended as she felt herself drawn into the glimmering depths of his eyes again. The beat of her pulse quickened. She forced herself to look away and murmured a thanks as he gathered the jacket around her.

"Got a car?"

She shook her head.

"Well, I've got mine parked down the trail a ways. I'll give you a lift home."

"No, no, that's all right," she said quickly. "I'm sure I can make it by myself."

He looked at her, a faint smile on his face. "I'm sure you could. But why freeze to death? Come on." He moved past her to the path and cocked his head, indicating she should walk ahead of him. Even though the sun was higher now, the air was icy on her skin. With a resigned shrug, she joined him on the trail.

She felt his eyes on her as he walked behind carrying her soggy sweater. She wished this jacket of his came down farther, to cover the rip in her pants. After a few yards, the trail was wide enough for them to walk side by side. Having him next to her made her just as self-conscious. When the wind came up, it seemed to go right through her. She couldn't stop her teeth from chattering. Her soaked sneakers squished with each step. The silence between them was making her even more uncomfortable.

"You're not from around here, are you?" she ventured.

"No," he said, and was silent. She was curious but didn't press him. She watched a squirrel whiz across the path. A crow cawed close by.

"You don't strike me as a college girl," he said, his voice low and caressing. "Or a local girl." He paused. "Or a housewife."

"I'm not married, if that's what you mean."

She hadn't said that. She couldn't possibly have. But she had, and she could sense him smiling.

"That wasn't exactly what I meant. But it's nice to know." His tone was even, pleasant, the words only mildly flirtatious, but his eyes were making her feel naked again. The air in the few feet that separated them was palpably electric. "Where do you come from?" he asked.

Why should I tell you? she thought, but she said: "Chicago, originally." She didn't know what to do with her arms. She put her hands in the pockets of his jacket.

"What are you doing in Silver Falls?"

"Teaching," she said. She didn't want to tell him anything more. She felt there was somehow too much intimacy between them already.

"Does teaching keep you busy?"

She cleared her throat. "Most of the time."

"What do you do the rest of the time?"

"You ask a lot of questions," she said.

"What are you doing for dinner tonight?"

She stopped walking and glared at him. But one look into those velvet eyes and she was spinning again.

"Thanks, but I'm busy," she managed to say.

"Lunch?"

She shook her head emphatically.

"Breakfast?"

"I don't really have time for breakfast," she said, and added pointedly: "As it is, I may be late for a faculty meeting."

"Ah. Sorry. I'm parked over here."

He gestured toward the opening in the forest up ahead where bright sunlight glimmered. The rays that filtered through the trees around them gave his face a tawny glow. Towering above her own five foot ten inches, he was undeniably a fabulous-looking man. Again she felt the power of his dark gaze as a titillating thread of desire coursed through her body. She turned, hoping that by avoiding his gaze her equilibrium would be restored.

"Where?" she asked.

In answer, he continued on. She was glad to see the end of the trail approaching. As they neared the clearing and emerged from the protective shadows of the forest, she squinted in the morning light.

"Over here," the man said, and she turned.

The car was a stunning vintage automobile in mint condition, an American beauty that had probably cost a minor fortune. Its color was a gleaming turquoise blue, and it had a spotless white top. Its silver chrome glittered in the sun; the white walls of the tires shone. Amanda, who had expected something more like a pickup truck, was stunned.

"I'm impressed," she told him, recovering. "What is it?"

"A Thunderbird," he said, and she could hear the pride in his voice. "It's a fifty-five."

She nodded. The Thunderbird was a bygone era's vision of perfection, its clean lines and smooth curves styled for speed and comfort. He opened the passenger door for her, and she slid in. He closed it and walked around to his side, keys jingling. The car was a two-seater, its light red benchseat pre-dating buckets. Amanda couldn't resist running her hand over the soft leather upholstery as he got in. He shut his door and reached for the ignition in one swift motion, and the motor rumbled to life.

Cowboys and farmhands didn't own vintage Thunderbirds, she mused. Who was this guy anyway? His hand paused on the shift. "Where would you like to go?" he asked pleasantly.

"Oh! Home," she said, and then, reddening slightly at his poker-faced nod, continued: "Take a left, here at Maple. I live on Clayton Road," she added, more as a test to see if he was familiar with the town. He continued to look at her expectantly, so she surmised he wasn't. "It's not far," she told him. "Follow Maple until you come to a stop sign. Then make another left."

He drove with one hand on the wheel. Outside her window, the spire of Deermount's Main Hall glinted by, and a row of dormitories festooned with piles of leaves. Amanda realized she was huddled almost against the door. She felt most comfortable there, not that she was comfortable at all. Her clothes were still dripping. The nearness of him seemed to stir up her blood. Sitting on the same seat with him was harder than walking alongside him in the open air.

"I hope I'm not ruining your leather seats," she said, attempting a light tone.

"Don't worry about it. I'm as wet as you, so I'll take full responsibility for damages—though I doubt there'll be any."

He smiled amiably, his eyes on the road. Looking at his attractive profile, she felt her curiosity increase. "Your first visit to Silver Falls?" she asked.

He nodded. "Have you lived here long?"

Once again he was volunteering no information about himself. "About eight years," she said slowly, and then:

"Where did you say you were from?"

"I didn't," he said. "New York."

New York? That didn't jibe with cowboy boots at all. She was about to ask him what he'd been doing in Silver Falls at sunrise when he turned the wheel sharply, looking out his side window. "Is this your block?"

It was. Clayton Street was resplendent in red, masses of crimson maple boughs waving at her in greeting. She pointed. "That driveway just past the big white house on the right."

Amanda lived alone in a suite of small rooms over a garage that had once belonged to the old Howard house next door. The man pulled the blue Thunderbird up to the curb by the driveway, and a few ruby leaves fell on the hood.

She was glad to see he kept the motor running. She didn't want to invite him up for a friendly cup of coffee. Things might get too friendly. And she did have a meeting to get to. She steeled herself and turned toward him, meeting his eyes directly at close range for the first time since her rescue on the river bank.

"Well," she began, once more finding it difficult to think clearly when they made eye contact. She had to keep herself from slipping into the grip of those soft brown orbs flecked with olive and gold. "Thank you. For, ah, helping me out."

"My pleasure." He held his hand out for her to shake. Amanda's pulse rose a notch. She supposed she was being ridiculous, but she somehow dreaded shaking his hand. Involuntarily, she wiped her hand on her hip, then reached out, fighting an absurd impulse to close her eyes.

Warmth. Power. He had a firm, hearty shake and a soft palm. She fixed her gaze dumbly on their hands, entwined like two old friends. She felt the intriguing heat from him and the answering flicker of her own desire.

Then his hand slipped from hers. She remembered suddenly that she still had his jacket gathered around her. She quickly wriggled out of it. As she patted it down on the seat between them and reached for her own sweater, he bent over, his face all at once only inches from hers. She froze.

His serene gaze caressed her features. "You may not be a Polar Bear," he said softly, "but if you don't mind my saying so . . . you're a very beautiful woman."

Amanda felt the hairs on the back of her neck tingle as, rooted to the spot, she felt his arm slide across the back of the seat. His slender fingers grazed her ear, gently twining a curl in her hair. And then, slowly, he brought his face even closer.

As his lips met hers, she felt their warm breath mingle. Then his mouth was melded to hers, and her blood rose, her skin pulsed to vibrant life. His tongue parted her lips, seeking her tongue, and she was filled with sensations so overwhelming she nearly fainted.

The tips of their tongues met, meshed. Deeper, sensual pulses of desire rose from lower in her trembling body. His kiss became more urgent, and her blood pounded in response. His hand moved to her waist, sliding gently upward over her ribs, his thumb grazing the swell of her breast. He pulled her closer. She felt the hardening points of her nipples strain against his chest through the thin wet fabric.

Then, alarmed by the intensity of her feelings, she pushed him away. She felt the beating of his heart beneath her outstretched palm and quickly recoiled her hand as if she'd been burnt. She felt her own heart pounding as she struggled to regain her composure, trying to will the color from her blazing cheeks. She didn't want him to know how much fevered, yearning excitement their kiss had aroused in her.

"No harm intended," he said quietly, watching her. "No harm done, I hope."

Amanda exhaled a deep breath. "I've got to go," she told him, eyes cast downward. She felt like she was itching all over, from inside out. It wasn't the wet clothes.

"You might want to clean that cut on your ankle with some alcohol," he said, and leaned back in his seat, hand ready on the gearshift.

"Right," she murmured. She opened the door, clambered out quickly, and shut it behind her. The man gunned his motor.

"Stay dry," he called to her through the window. Then he pulled the T-bird from the curb, gliding off down Clayton Street in a gust of leaves.

Her lips quivering, Amanda watched the car until she could no longer see it. When the sound of the motor buzzed into the distance, fading, and there was only the persistent rustle of tree branches above her, she stirred, as if waking from a dream.

She realized two things simultaneously: that she was freezing to death, and that she didn't even know the man's name.

THE HOT WATER cascading over her neck and shoulders was luxurious after the icy discomfort of the morning. Amanda could have stood in the shower for an hour. But her meeting with Professor Hutchins and the dean was in twenty-five minutes, and she didn't want to be late. Moments later she was toweling her freshly shampooed hair. After quickly wiping steam from the mirror in her little bathroom, she dabbed on some pale rose eye shadow and brushed on a touch of mascara.

She didn't use much makeup as a rule. A fortunate accident of birth had given her delicate, classical features that needed no accent. Her eyes were large, and their color startling—as her rescuer had noted. Her nose was fine-boned and slender, with a soft, rounded tip. She wasn't crazy about the little dimple in her chin, but past admirers had claimed to be—and Amanda supposed it was all a matter of taste. But she couldn't complain about her prominent cheekbones or her full, sensual lips.

Now she brought out the natural touch of color in her cheeks with some blush-on and finished with a shade of vermilion lipstick. Picking up a brush, she quickly combed her wavy tresses back from her forehead. A curl of bangs bounced into place over her left eyebrow, covering the thin, arching line. It gave her face a faintly sultry look, the body of her long black hair framing her fair skin as it fell past her shoulders.

Professors of English Literature weren't usually as attractive as Amanda. Generally, some deep-rooted feminist side of her nature prevented her from playing up her natural assets too obviously, yet this morning she thought it was important to look her best. The dean, a known womanizer, had a weakness for fashionable females. His was the final decision in choosing an artist for the summer residency at Deermount, and she needed all the influence she could muster with him. She was pushing for her favorite poet, Sherman McGuinness. As he wasn't a stylish celebrity, she knew it would be an uphill battle.

Amanda had earned her Ph.D by writing a dissertation on McGuinness. If the poet came to Deermount, she believed she could win his approval of her critical study on his work, and her chances for getting it published (usually one in a thousand) would then increase dramatically. A published book on McGuinness sanctioned by the illustrious man himself was the kind of coup that would make her reputation in the academic community.

And so she had picked out a dress that was sheer and form-fitting, a deep maroon silk with a neckline that was eye-catching without being too risqué. Amanda moved into her bedroom, slipped on a pair of stockings, and then the dress. She chose high heels, which she rarely wore on campus, to enhance her lean legs and increase her already dramatic stature. Simple, small silver earrings completed the outfit. She checked herself out in the full-length mirror on the back of her closet door.

The bare shoulders were too much, she decided. She returned to her closet for her black linen jacket, and that seemed to do the trick. The padded shoulders seemed to harden her lines somewhat, giving her an air of businesslike formality. Satisfied at last, Amanda let herself out of the house.

The click of her heels echoed down Clayton Street. It was less than a five-minute walk to her faculty building on campus, but she kept up a brisk pace. Ahead, the sun parted some gray clouds, turning the tree tops into a shimmering riot of color. Everything around her looked crisp and vibrant, from the silver pinpoints of dew on the grass along the curb to the speckled slate shingles on the quiet, quaint houses she passed.

She used to think towns like Silver Falls existed only in the remote past, or on TV. Her first semester here, she'd half-expected to see Beaver Cleaver whiz by on his bike, or Ozzie Nelson out mowing his lawn. It was an old, family community. The only concession it had made to the constant influx of students was that on Saturday nights the bakery on Main Street stayed open late.

By her first summer, Amanda was used to the idea that children actually sold lemonade on street corners, and she was in love with the place. She felt more of a sense of belonging here than she'd ever felt in the indifferent suburb where she'd grown up. She'd always been a loner; without any brothers and sisters, family had been only Dad, her mother having died when Amanda was four years old. In Silver Falls, she could vicariously enjoy a full spectrum of family life, from young mothers with their unruly broods, causing traffic jams in the local supermarket aisles to sleepy grandfathers soaking up sun in the town square. She liked to pretend she was a part of it all.

The wind rose. She pulled her jacket closed. You're still an outsider, she reminded herself. You're most at ease when all those family folks are asleep in their beds and you walk the street alone.

But there had been a time when she'd felt that feeling of belonging for real—a wonderful, precious time. There was a name she was best off forgetting; a face she always felt the worse for contemplating. But in the way one's tongue can't help nudging around a painful cavity, Amanda's thoughts inevitably turned to Brad.

Well, there was progress, she mused ruefully. Not all that long ago, Brad Sonders—or the absence of him— had been in her thoughts constantly. Now his presence there was unexpected, like a sudden cloud covering the sun on what had been a lovely day. She tried to picture her former lover, and one-time fiancé, as someone she didn't know, hadn't known so intimately.

Funny, but the first image that came to her was the "head shot" he used with his acting résumé: Brad smiling, his almost too-handsome face a model of composure, with perfect white teeth and blond hair shining. The camera liked him, as it was said in the trade. And ultimately, his love affair with the lens had eclipsed his love for Amanda. He'd left Silver Falls, choosing movie roles in Hollywood over a life with her.

It would be too easy to rekindle the bitterness. She fought it off, as well as the sweet memories that had a sting to them. Her heart tested the fiber of its tenderest regions, feeling for the edges of the old wound to see how well it had healed.

But a more present soreness overrode those thoughts. Her ankle was throbbing. Amanda paused at the edge of the campus green to inspect the Band-Aid beneath her stocking. Suddenly she thought of the man in the Glen. She remembered his strong but gentle touch melting her skin, his burning lips...She realized that thoughts of the stranger had hovered around her all morning—an outside, fuzzy excitement, like on Friday afternoons, when she knew the weekend was about to begin. Unconsciously, she'd avoided thinking about him directly, as though saving it for later, and she was surprised at the elation his memory inspired. She wondered if they would ever meet again.

The ivy-lined bell tower of the library across campus tolled eight. It was just like Professor Hutchins to plan their meeting at an hour in the morning when most faculty members would be having leisurely breakfasts. The crotchety senior chairman of the Fine Arts Department would no doubt grumble if she was one minute late. Amanda hurried into the red brick archway of the West Building and headed for its rickety staircase.

She'd been hoping to have a few minutes alone with Hutchins to restate her case for McGuinness before the dean joined them. But when Mrs. White, the professor's secretary, ushered her into his office, she saw that the dean had already arrived. Both men rose politely from their seats as she entered, Professor Hutchins furrowing his bushy white eyebrows at his pocketwatch, true to form. He gave her a perfunctory nod before muttering an introduction and sinking back into his chair behind the large ebony desk.

"Miss Farr? I don't believe we've met before," the dean said congenially, shaking her hand. His grip was almost painfully firm, his smile expansive beyond the call of duty. Dean Chast was part of the new breed of academia at Deermount. Younger and more handsome than his predecessors, he resembled a television newscaster more than a man of learning. He was tall and perennially tanned, with a square jaw, high forehead, and boundless enthusiasm radiating from his dark eyes. He welcomed all things modern to his "ever-expanding" liberal arts college, had recently computerized the library, and was beginning to offer courses at Deermount that Amanda found superficial and trendy. At the moment, he was taking in her attire with more than professorial interest.

Amanda removed her hand. "Do sit down," the dean boomed. She took a chair not far from his that faced Professor Hutchins. Hutchins ran his knobby fingers through his white beard and grimaced towards the silver tea set on his desk.

"There's tea if you like."

"No, thank you." She crossed her legs and glanced at the antique furnishings in the room, conscious of the dean's eyes still upon her.

"Professor Hutchins tells me you have suggested a candidate for the summer residency," he said.

"Yes. Sherman McGuinness."

"The poet?" He turned to Hutchins. "Isn't that the fellow who's speaking here next week?"

"Yes," Amanda said, as Hutchins nodded. She'd practically twisted the arm of the Speaker Committee's chairman to get the poet booked for a reading. "He's one of the finest contemporary poets in this country," she went on. "I wrote my dissertation on him, and I'm currently expanding it into a book. He's won accolade after accolade. I know he'd be a real asset to the residency program—"

"But what has he done?" the dean interrupted.

"Done?" repeated Amanda, a bit thrown by the question. "Well, he's published a great many books of verse. He's being anthologized right and left these days, and he recently won the Robert Frost Memorial Medal..." She continued, listing the man's various honors, which she'd memorized during her many years of research on the man. Relief flooded through her as she spoke; surely the dean was more apt to be swayed by a recital of the man's awards than an impassioned appraisal of his work.

But she soon became aware that the dean was not really listening to her. His attention was on her body, his eyes perusing her slowly. She began to wonder now if she'd made a mistake in her selection of dress. She wanted the dean to be interested in what she had to say, not just in what she had on.

"Impressive credits," he said when she'd concluded her pitch, but something in his tone indicated that he was sincerely underwhelmed. "Very impressive," he repeated, leaning forward, fixing his eyes on hers. This time Amanda had the distinct impression he was referring to her physical attributes. "But this Herman McGuinness—"

"Sherman," she corrected, and the dean's eyes twinkled.

"Sherman McGuinness," he said with exaggerated politeness. "Sounds more like an ale than a poet," he added with a smile at Hutchins. Hutchins chuckled complacently. Amanda fought an irrational impulse to reach over the desk and pull his beard out by the roots. She was used to the male camaraderie among colleagues at Deermount; she was one of the few women in her department and had had to struggle to get the position. But she still resented not being taken seriously by two men who should have been above such chauvinism.

"As you may realize, Miss Farr," said the dean, folding his hands in his lap, "The summer residency is an important element in the survival of our program. Though I may say I've had good luck getting funding in the past..." He paused here to allow his self-congratulatory phrase to sink in. "...finding funds each year is a delicate business. The summer residency is, as they say, a draw. I, for one, feel that its drawing power is enhanced by the selection of a very visible, well-known personage. Your Mr. McGuinness is fairly obscure."

"In some circles, I suppose," Amanda started, feeling her blood roil. "But isn't the point of such a program the exposure it gives students to the kind of artistry they wouldn't find on television?"

Even as she said this she sensed she'd gone too far. The dean's face darkened. "How long have you been with us?" he asked, with a faintly menacing cordiality.

"This is my second year teaching," she replied. The dean put his hands palms up in the air, as if that was all that need be said.

"Miss Farr is one of our exceptional cases," rumbled Professor Hutchins. Amanda was surprised to hear him come to her defense. "It's not often that we allow a student to stay on and join the faculty. But she has proven herself a worthy addition." He smiled at her and then the dean, and Amanda comprehended that he was covering for himself as well as for her. The dean nodded, his expression once more benign.

"I'm sure she has," he said, looking at her meaningfully. "But at any rate, Miss Farr, high visibility is the important factor. In light of this, we already have our eye on what may be a most fortuitous selection for the residency—Ethan Taylor."

Amanda stifled an exclamation of disappointment. Ethan Taylor was exactly the sort of celebrity Dean Chast would covet. He was a commercially successful playwright, whose pretensions to seriousness had earned him the Pultizer Prize a few years back. Although she wasn't very familiar with the man's work, and didn't want to be, Brad and his circle had idolized Taylor. Brad had wanted to do a production of his most famous play at

Deermount, the one with the odd, pretentious title—what
was it?—*Cry of the Dakota Angels*.

"Oh, yes," she managed to say. "The popular playwright."

"The Pulitzer Prize-winning playwright," said the
dean, with reverence. "His latest production is being
mounted in New York—on Broadway—even as we
speak."

"They call him the 'Golden Boy of the American
Stage,'" said Hutchins. "No one's blazed such a meteoric
trail through theatrical circles since Tennessee Williams."

Amanda suddenly realized that Hutchins had known
about this all along. He'd merely been placating her when
he'd agreed to bring her proposal up with the dean. You
old jackass, she thought bitterly, you'd welcome Evel
Knievel to the campus for a course on motorcycle stunts
if you thought it would please Dean Chast.

"In fact, Mr. Taylor has already expressed an interest," the dean continued. "We've invited him to visit the
campus, as he wishes to look over the facilities of our
Theater Department before making a decision."

Amanda played her last card. "Sherman McGuinness
is speaking here this coming Tuesday," she reminded
him. "Perhaps after the reading you could meet him and
assess his strengths as a teacher yourself."

The dean nodded. "That sounds like a fine idea," he
said. "It wouldn't hurt to have a back-up possibility. As
it is, we're meeting Ethan Taylor this morning. I expect
him in my office momentarily."

He beamed at Amanda like the proverbial cat who'd
swallowed the canary. She pursed her lips, trying not to
emit a groan of frustration. It was bad enough that some
Broadway buffoon was likely to nip her plans in the bud.

But she also had a feeling that the presence of a famous theatrical hack on campus would turn the summer residency program into more of a circus than an educational experience.

"It was good of him to take some time away from the Great White Way to visit our little university, don't you think?" the dean was saying to Hutchins.

"Quite," said the old man. Amanda felt her hackles rising. In her view, the Great White Way—home of the dubious "rock musical"—hadn't exhibited anything worthy of serious attention since Eugene O'Neill. And if Ethan Taylor was anything like some of Brad's friends in the Drama Workshop, she could expect the worst. Her exposure to those superficially sensitive pretty-boy actors and those ostentatious, swelled-headed actresses had left a bad taste in her mouth whenever "theater people" were concerned.

The door to Professor Hutchins's office opened. Mrs. White peered in. "Excuse me, Dean Chast. There's a Mr. Taylor to see you."

"Ah, what timing! You may as well send him in here," the dean declared.

Amanda formed a mental picture of the awaited "Golden Boy": lots of jewelry, shirt half-unbuttoned to reveal gold chains, carefully coiffed hair, and designer jeans. Or was he the "serious" type, with soulful eyes magnified by horn-rimmed glasses, and patches on his elbows?

But nothing in her imagination prepared her for the man who walked through the door. The tips of his boots were no longer splattered with mud, and he'd put on a worn corduroy jacket over his flannel shirt, but there was no mistaking Ethan Taylor. He was the man who had pulled her from the Silver River a few hours ago, held her in his arms, and with one kiss ignited a passion in her that she'd never experienced before.

He strode into the room, his powerful, rangy form eclipsing the dean as they shook hands. Amanda felt as though she were looking at him through the wrong end of a telescope. The room had turned into a tunnel around her, the end of it focused on the man's luminous, piercing eyes. He turned his glistening gaze on her now. Her heart skipped a beat and nearly stopped altogether. As if from a great distance, she heard the dean introducing her. She put out her hand to grip Ethan's and was relieved to see that hers wasn't shaking like a leaf.

"Hi there," he said, taking her hand, his face registering surprised recognition. Aware of a soft jolt within her at his touch, Amanda felt the blood rise in her cheeks and was only able to nod a response, her mind reeling. She'd been prepared to hate Ethan Taylor on sight. Now she had to reconcile her image of a Pulitzer Prize-winning habitué of Broadway with the rugged, outdoors type she'd mistaken for a farmhand in the Glen. With his hand grasping hers, she could barely think at all.

"Miss Farr is a professor here at Deermount," Hutchins was saying.

"Really?" Ethan said, his eyes still upon her, traveling swiftly over her dress. Goosebumps rose on the skin of her arms. She felt her body strain subtly in her clothing, the tips of her breasts swelling and tingling at the brief but intimate caress of his gaze. She wondered if he was trying to find the soaked and bedraggled girl he'd embraced on the river bank in the stylishly attired young woman standing before him.

He let go of her hand at last. "What do you teach, Professor?" he asked with a mischievous smile. "Physical ed?"

"Poetry," she said, bridling at his flip insinuation. "English literature." He was still smiling, and she had the distinct impression he was enjoying her predicament.

It seemed he was about to say more, but the dean interrupted, pouring an obviously rehearsed speech of welcome in the playwright's ear. Ethan cocked his head, listening amiably, his eyes still on Amanda.

"Tea?" offered Professor Hutchins.

"No thanks," Ethan replied. Amanda watched him take in his surroundings for the first time. He looked as out of place in the musty, antiquated study as a cowboy in the House of Commons. He hooked his thumbs in his belt loops, his eyes, with an expression of amused incredulity, roving over the cases of leather-bound tomes that lined the walls. He looked back at Amanda. He was scrutinizing her appearance, as if trying to place her in the context of the room's stuffy atmosphere.

"I'm sure you'll want to meet Professor Collins," the dean said. "He's expecting us over at the little amphitheater where our young thespians strain and toil in their efforts to summon up the Muse. I think you'll find the facilities quite charming, albeit somewhat threadbare."

Ethan Taylor appeared to find the dean's pontifications entertaining. He smiled at him, bending one ear forward slightly with his fingers, as if he were examining the timbre of some foreign dialect.

"If you've got a stage big enough for a guy my size to walk across it without falling off, maybe I can do something with it," he said.

The dean chuckled, and Hutchins sputtered out a laugh that was more like a cough.

"It's twenty-five feet across and eighteen deep," Amanda said dryly. She thought she'd detected a trace of smugness in his attitude. If Ethan expected her to be bowled over by the revelation of his celebrated status, she'd prove him wrong. "Most of the students aren't quite as big as you are, Mr. Taylor, but they manage quite nicely."

He turned toward her, eyes glittering with enlivened interest. "You're familiar with the Theater Department, Miss Farr?"

"To be honest, I'm familiar enough to have had my fill of it."

"Then you don't see much theater these days?"

"I'd rather read a book," she said.

"Well," said the dean preemptively, shooting her an annoyed look. "Shall we join Professor Collins?" He was about to put his hand on Ethan's shoulder in a gesture of unearned familiarity, but thought better of it as the taller man turned to look at him.

"Sure," said Ethan. He walked to the door with the dean, then turned back to nod a good-bye at Hutchins. Then he addressed Amanda. "See you 'round campus," he said with a roguish wink. Before she could compose herself for a reply, he was gone.

It was maddening that the man thought he could stroll into her school—and her heart—so nonchalantly as if both precious things could be his just for the asking. She glared at the door that swung shut behind the two men. Only when Professor Hutchins cleared his throat in back of her did she remember she wasn't alone.

"Handsome fellow," Hutchins commented, eyeing her inquisitively. She wondered if he'd picked up on the electricity she'd felt between Ethan and herself, or the hint of familiarity he'd indicated before leaving. The professor pulled out his pocketwatch and wound it. "Well," he said, "I have some papers that need attending to . . ."

Amanda strode up to his desk, more resolved than ever to continue her push for McGuinness. She didn't like the idea of Ethan Taylor having the run of the campus, and the thought of his continued presence in her vicinity was alarming. He made her feel too vulnerable, too out of control; he made her feel . . . too much.

"Look, Professor," she said. "You know as well as I do that the sum value of Sherman McGuinness's work is worth more than all the Ethan Taylors in the world! Why, you even wrote a monograph on his poetry yourself."

"Yes, I did, didn't I?" Hutchins murmured vaguely, stroking his beard. "Well, Miss Farr, as the dean said, there'd be no harm in following up on him. If you wish to introduce him to the dean on Tuesday, you have my support. At the very least, it would be an honor and a pleasure to have him in residence at Deermount."

"Thank you," Amanda said stiffly, and still bristling at the complacency of Hutchins and all men, she left the dusty study.

Her English Lit. 101 course was impossible that morning. She couldn't keep her mind on her work, which was ironic, as it was usually her students whose concentration wandered. More than once, she mis-heard or completely missed a question from the class. Her inner vision was repeatedly invaded by images of Ethan, his eyes, his smiling lips. She found herself drawn to the window that overlooked the Main Lawn. Realizing that she was scanning each passing figure to see if it was Ethan, and infuriated at her own school-girlish preoccupation with the man, she slammed a copy of John Milton down on the windowsill, frightening a freshman co-ed seated nearby out of her wits.

Thankfully, it was her only class of the day. Amanda

walked across campus to her office, trying to focus her thoughts on academic matters. But once again, she found herself musing upon Ethan Taylor. Some dim remembrance of him was troubling her. She vaguely recalled that he'd been associated with some other famous figure in the theater world—a woman...

Why such a thing should concern, let alone bother her was beyond imagining. With an exasperated sigh, Amanda entered the West Building. Once inside her tiny office upstairs she welcomed, for a change, the chance to lose herself in the stack of papers on her desk. She grabbed a sophomore's treatise on Keats that looked more neatly typed than most and dove in.

Sphinx, the fat black cat-in-residence of the building, rubbed his furry girth against her leg. Amanda gave his back a brief scratch. When she removed her hand, he kept his behind up and looked at her with a mildly astonished gaze, as if to say, "That's all?" Seeing no reprise of affection forthcoming, Sphinx padded across the room and sat, staring moodily at the doorway. Then his green eyes widened, and his ears stood up.

"You look just as good with your hair dry," said a familiar voice. Amanda whirled around in her chair. Ethan Taylor was leaning against the open door to the office, arms folded. "Hope I'm not interrupting," he added as he walked up to her desk. "Mind if I come in?"

"You're already in," she noted, trying to keep a close rein on her emotions as her body shivered at his approach. His mellifluous voice was already fogging up her mind. "Well, Mr. Taylor, have you seen what you came to see?"

"More than I'd hoped to, actually," he answered, turning the full force of his seductive eyes upon her.

Amanda deliberately ignored his innuendo. "Then

you'll be going shortly, won't you?"

Ethan shook his head. "Not just yet, no. Not until I've taken you to dinner tonight."

Amanda's eyes widened. "As I remember, we decided against making any date," she said sharply.

"Well, I guess I was hoping that since we'd been more formally introduced, you'd reconsider. Where would you like to go?"

"Nowhere." She stood up, heart beating loudly. She strode quickly away from the nearness of him to the doorway. Sphinx followed. The cat paused at her side to give Ethan a haughty stare, then sauntered off down the hall, tail high.

"You may be used to impressing the women of New York City so easily that they run off with you at the drop of a hat," she said dryly, "but *I* have a big load of work to deal with here at our little college. I'm afraid I won't be able to fit you in."

"I wish you would," he said. Instead of imbuing the words with the insolence they might have had, he made it such a simple, humble request that her heart throbbed faster. She was exasperated.

"Listen," he continued. "I know a place not far from here that serves home-style cooking that'll make your mouth water. With my car, the whole thing wouldn't take up more than an hour of your time."

Amanda shook her head. Ethan sighed, seeming genuinely perplexed by her resistance. "Is it something I said?" His look was quizzical. "It's not who I am, is it?" he ventured, eyes narrowing. She didn't answer. Ethan rubbed his cheek thoughtfully. "Maybe I'm being a little forward, but—"

"It seems to be your nature."

"—is there someone else?"

She gave him her coolest stare. "I don't see why it's any of your business, but the answer to your question— to *all* your questions—is no."

Ethan paced a slow half-circle around her. "Let me get this straight," he said, as though explicating a complex mathematical problem. "You're passing up the prospect of a free meal, the glory of a vintage T-bird on the open highway, and the company of a man who was willing to join you in an ice-cold bath at an ungodly hour of the morning out of sheer contrariness?"

She smiled in spite of herself, swayed by the look of earnest indignation on his face. But she was liking him too much already. Hadn't she learned by now that charming men with the theater in their blood were most likely one-way tickets to disaster? After the last one, she was more than wary.

"It's a decent offer," she admitted. "But I'll have to turn it down."

The boyish look evaporated from his face. "That's a shame," he said quietly. The silence between them was loud with the unspoken. Then he moved closer, put a warm hand on her shoulder, and gazed steadily into her eyes.

"Listen, Amanda," he said. The husky urgency in his voice touched a chord deep inside her and made it resonate. "I don't know what kind of a man you imagine me to be, but I'll tell you—casual flirtations are not my idea of a good time. I want you to come to dinner with me because I like you. And I don't quite understand your resistance to such a harmless invitation."

"Harmless?"

"If you're thinking about this morning, I want you to know I don't regret it—and you shouldn't either. But if kissing a stranger rubbed you the wrong way..." An

impish smile was forming at the corners of his mouth.
". . . I'm willing to wait until you get to know me a little
better."

Amanda looked at him, both irked by his insolence
and charmed by his directness. She considered the consequences of a night out with the Golden Boy of the
American Stage. If he was on the level, maybe there was
an interesting person beneath the arrogance, and at the
least she'd be entertained. If he wasn't . . . Well, it could
be one for the memoirs.

"Does wine come with the meal?"

He smiled. "Absolutely."

"All right," she said slowly. "You've convinced me."

He gave her shoulder a quick, deft squeeze. "I'll pick
you up at half past seven. I remember where you live."

She nodded. He nodded. Then he turned and walked
out of her office. Amanda sank into the wicker chair by
her desk. Now that he was gone, what had appeared to
be a moment of clarity seemed more like a moment of
madness.

Sphinx padded back into the room and sat on his
haunches a few feet away. He looked up at her, his
whiskers quivering.

"Sphinx," she said, "what am I getting myself into?"

The cat demurely closed its eyes and purred.

Chapter

3

AMANDA STOPPED IN at the Student Union on her way home. She was curious to know how the tickets for Sherman McGuinness's upcoming poetry reading were selling at the box office.

The Union was fairly deserted at the end of this Friday afternoon. A few students lounged on the brightly colored couches that lined its off-white concrete walls. After the jarring events of the day, Amanda found the quiet atmosphere of the lobby soothingly familiar. As she crossed the parquet floor to the box office booth, her mind drifted to thoughts of a faculty meeting she was scheduled to attend the following week. So she was quite unprepared for the shock of suddenly confronting Ethan Taylor's serene gaze.

He stared down at her in radiant black and white from the back of an oversized paperback propped up in the booth's window. Amanda waited for her pulse and breathing to return to normal before knocking on the glass.

A pale, round, bespectacled face peered over the book at her. Amanda recognized Deborah Varrone, a student in one of her classes. A walking contradiction of the fat-equals-jolly cliché, Deborah was as dour as she was rotund. She rarely spoke in class, but Amanda had recently graded a paper of hers on John Donne that revealed a personality sunk deep in sophomoric philosophical despair.

"How's the McGuinness reading doing?" Amanda asked.

"Poorly," Deborah soberly informed her. "Things may pick up by Tuesday, but I doubt we'll sell out. I think it's a reflection of the intellectual apathy of our times."

Amanda actually shared that view, but had to suppress a smile at the girl's painful earnestness. She turned to go, having learned what she needed to know, but stopped, unable to resist asking Deborah with studied casualness, "Are you enjoying your book?"

"I believe," the girl reverently intoned, "that no other playwright has ever captured the dark underside of contemporary culture with such vivid insightfulness." She looked down at Ethan's photo, shaking her head. "Such a beautiful man..." she sighed. "And such a tragic figure."

Tragic? It was the last word Amanda would have associated with the arrogant, cheekily good-humored man who had just wrangled a dinner date. "What do you mean?"

Deborah's eyes ballooned behind her thick glasses. "You've heard the story, haven't you? About Sono Araki?"

She had, she realized suddenly. Sono Araki—that was the name of the woman associated with Ethan she'd been trying to recall earlier. She remembered hearing about the incident a while back, when she was still with Brad. Sono had been a famous theatrical set designer—and Ethan Taylor's wife. Shortly after he won the Pulitzer, she had died...

"Yes, of course," Amanda said. "His wife."

"They say he still hasn't recovered," Deborah said.

"The two of them were so close..."

"It was just two years ago, wasn't it?" Amanda said carefully. "How did she—?"

"Sleeping pills," Deborah said, lowering her voice. "An overdose." She leaned forward with a conspiratorial air. "I don't believe that gossip in the papers. They never proved it was a suicide—after all, officially it was an accident."

"Suicide?" Amanda repeated, feeling a momentary chill in the lobby's cavernous interior.

"I don't believe Ethan Taylor had anything to do with Araki's death," said Deborah solemnly. "He's much too sensitive a man to have mistreated her—don't you think?"

"No," Amanda said, drawing back. "I mean, yes," she added quickly. "Well! Thank you for the information..." With a brusque wave good-bye to Deborah, she hurriedly rushed from the ticket booth, aware that she was acting foolishly, but eager to be back in the open air. Outside, she paused on the Union steps and took a deep breath.

She tried to picture this man she barely knew as a mournful figure who was possibly responsible for his wife's suicide. It was difficult. She could only visualize, vividly, the healthy glow of Ethan's smiling face. Amanda considered then the source for this bit of gossip. What could a college girl like Deborah Varrone know about Ethan Taylor, anyway? It was probably a lot of melodramatic nonsense.

But what do *you* know, really? queried a little demon in her mind. Ethan's charming sincerity might be the mask of a heel on the make, with a closetful of skeletons in his past. Amanda sighed. The man was beginning to seem maddeningly complex. Why was he interested in her, anyway? And why did he have to be so...

Attractive. And powerfully arousing, more so than any man she'd ever known; it was undeniable. All the more reason, she decided as she walked up the stairs to her apartment, to get him out of her life before he ruined it.

But backing out of the date would be adolescent cowardice. Her mission—and she chose to accept it, realizing that her cancellation might inflame the man's persistence—was to somehow convince Ethan Taylor, whoever he was, to forget about the summer residency at Deermount.

Amanda inspected the one-piece black dress she'd pulled from the selection laid out upon her bed. It had an elegant simplicity...and a provocative slit up one side. As she debated its merits, standing in her bra and half-slip, she reviewed her plan of attack. Brad had told her many horror stories about the theater department's inadequacies. She knew the budget for the residency was paltry, knew the shortcomings of the staff—was this enough to give the playwright second thoughts?

There was the sound of a car pulling up outside. Damn. Her dawdling had made her late, but her date, according to the clock, was right on time.

Holding the dress in front of her half-naked form, she went to the window overlooking the driveway. Directly below her was the hood of the infamous Thunderbird. Ethan opened the door and sprang from his seat like some lithe and graceful mountain lion. She watched as he shut the door and, thinking himself unobserved, smoothed back his hair, his face shining with buoyant anticipation.

Amanda raised the window and leaned over the sill. "I'll be right down," she called. When his face brightened further at the sound of her voice and he smiled, something moved inside of her. She turned quickly from the window. She'd detected subtle signs of his having spruced himself up a bit—a shave, a fresh, light-blue cotton shirt beneath the corduroy jacket—but he still had that tousled, woodsy air about him that she was beginning to find so appealing. Careful, she warned herself: Proceed with extreme caution. Keep a clear head at all times.

Five minutes later she was sliding into the passenger side of the car, her dress still warm from the iron. Ethan's admiring gaze swiftly swept her from head to foot. The sensual gleam in his dark eyes excited her. Her quickened breathing caused the soft globes of her breasts to rise and fall under the clinging material. The clear head was already clouding.

"Could you put your eyes on low-beam?" she asked.

He smiled. "I'm sorry, Professor. And I promise you, I'll keep both hands on the steering wheel."

"Good," she replied. "I promise that this time I won't drip remnants of the Silver River on your nice upholstery." Ethan chuckled and eased the T-bird down the driveway.

She decided it was best to waste no time. "What did you think of the Theater Department?" she asked.

"Not much," he said, turning onto Oak Street.

"And Professor Collins?"

"Pig-headed bore."

Amanda smiled. So far, so good. "Then you're reconsidering taking the dean up on his offer?"

Ethan squinted in the orange rays of the setting sun. "Yes . . ." He paused. ". . . and no." Amanda thought she saw the trace of a smile on his lips. She had a sneaking suspicion she was being played with.

"What is it about Deermount that interests you, then?" she pressed, determined to open him up.

He glanced at her briefly, then returned his eyes to the road, shaking his head in mock dismay. "You wouldn't like my answer to that question."

"Never mind," she said wryly, getting the message and facing front herself.

They were out of Silver Falls already, gliding through the open meadows and fields that surrounded the town. She was content for the moment to watch the slow, dramatic descent of the sun on the horizon. The sky was a technicolor vista of purplish clouds, with the silver line of highway at its center. Ethan's window was open. The wind blew her hair up behind her like a dark halo. It was an exhilarating sensation. But the cold air suddenly reminded her of the morning, when she'd been a huddled bunch of soaked nerves in this same seat. Amanda shivered as she inwardly winced.

"Too much for you?"

"No, it's all right."

He rolled the window up nonetheless. They had both been speaking loudly to be heard over the whistling of the wind. Now there was just the engine's hum. Amanda felt her body pulse softly with the subdued excitement she always seemed to feel in Ethan's presence. She forced herself to concentrate. "Did you get a look at the lighting board in the amphitheater?"

He shook his head.

"It's a relic," she went on. "It blows fuses every time a show goes up. They'll never replace it, though."

"Why not?"

"Not enough money in the budget. You see, the whole Theater Department is sort of a bastard child at Deermount. It's never been taken seriously, and all the equipment is ancient hand-me-downs..."

She continued to regale him with her negatively slanted

stories as they followed the winding highway through the sunset hills. Ethan listened thoughtfully for a while, then rather abruptly pulled the car off the road into a gravel parking lot. He leaned back in his seat and stared at her, the motor idling.

"Why do I get the distinct feeling that you don't want me to teach at Deermount next summer?"

"Because frankly I don't," she said.

"Why's that?"

"I had someone a lot more qualified in mind."

He raised his eyebrows. "I see. Such as?"

"There's a poet—I doubt you'd have heard of him—Sherman McGuinness."

"'Oh, the sundered lilies/the tiny spheres of pinpoint brilliance/flattened by Metropolis and Wheel...' That guy?"

She nodded, dumbfounded.

"A little on the dry side, but I guess he'll do," Ethan mused. "What makes you think I'm not qualified?"

She cleared her throat. "I didn't suppose that a Broadway playwright—"

"I didn't start out there, you know," he said, annoyed. "What have you got against theater, anyway?

"What do you see in teaching?" she countered. "You certainly don't need the money—not that there's much in it."

"Do you think I'm rich?"

"Aren't you?"

"I do all right." Ethan looked at her. "I take it you think that writers should starve, then?"

"Most serious writers have a hard time finding an audience," she said.

"So," he said with a faint smile. "Besides the fact that I'm a supposedly uneducated writer who's committed the sin of making money with his work, what else about me bothers you, Professor?"

Amanda glared at him, embarrassed by his patient perusal of her reddening face. "I thought we were on our way to dinner," she said.

"We're here," he announced.

"Where?" she asked. They were parked at the side of a long redwood building that looked more like a barn than a restaurant.

"Molly's," Ethan said, turning off the motor and getting out. A neon sign hanging at the far end of the building blinked, MOLLY'S TAVERN. As he opened the door for her, Amanda tried to mask her bewilderment, noting that the only other cars in the small lot were an old Chevy and a beat-up pickup truck.

"You can tell me what else is wrong with me over a bottle of wine," he said, helping her out of the car.

Over the crunch of her heels on the gray gravel, she heard soft strains of country and western music from within, and she could smell charcoal-broiled chicken. Ethan paused at the door, sensing her apprehension.

"This joint may not look like much, but the food's great."

"I'm just sorry I didn't wear my overalls," she said dryly.

"Glad you didn't," he answered as he held the door open. "Though I'm sure you'd look good in overalls, too." He followed her into the dimly lit interior where at first she saw only a long bar inhabited by a few burly-looking men in shirt-sleeves. As Ethan guided her down the sawdust-littered floor and her eyes adjusted to the subdued light, she saw more: a row of old-fashioned, high-backed booths along the other wall, with red and white checkered tablecloths and candles in red waxed glass holders. At the end of the room stood an ancient, majestic Wurlitzer jukebox gleaming blue and gold. A mournful Hank Williams tune wafted from it through the smoky air.

She didn't know what she'd expected—maybe something fancier, like a country inn with a genteel atmosphere—but she might have known that Ethan Taylor would opt for the unusual—and the homegrown—in tone. She slid into the booth he indicated and looked around her. She had to admit the unpretentious room had its charm. There were little white curtains on the windows, quaint paintings of country scenes on the pinewood walls, and the requisite moose head over the bar. She looked at Ethan. Elbows on the table, chin propped in his palms, he was watching her take in their surroundings, his face glowing red in the candlelight. She sensed he was awaiting her verdict.

"So it's not the Four Seasons," she said. "How's the barbecued chicken?"

His eyes sparkled. "Molly's specialty," he said. Amanda had a feeling she'd passed a subtle test: She could be as "down-home" as he obviously liked to be, despite his renown.

A large, stocky, gray-haired woman in an apron trundled up to their table. She greeted Ethan familiarly, and he kidded with her as he ordered their dinner—chicken for Amanda and a steak for himself, with a bottle of red wine. When the wine arrived, Ethan poured them each a glass, then sat back as she took a sip, examining her face again.

"We were discussing my lack of qualifications," he offered.

"Look," she said. "I'm sorry. You just didn't strike me as the academic type. And your reputation—"

"You don't look like the kind of person one would expect to find buried in the stuffy depths of academia yourself," he said. "Well?"

"I spent most of my childhood with my nose buried in a book," she told him. "I wore braces, and I used big words for my age."

"The braces paid off."

"So did the books. I was a teenage Shakespeare addict. I got to Deermount on a scholarship, and I liked it here, so I stayed on. It's not so stuffy, and I don't feel buried. That answer your question?"

He was gazing at her raptly, seeming to listen to more than her words. "Yes and no. It seems to me it would take more than a good teaching position to keep a woman like Amanda Farr cloistered in a small town in the wilds of the Midwest. Who was he?"

"Who was who?" She felt herself coloring. Damn the man! How could he seem to know her so well when he barely knew her at all? She took another sip of wine, determined to feign nonchalance.

"Well, you said yourself you weren't married, and you're not involved now..." He sipped his wine, then sat back again, his eyes still intent on her face. "... but you seem to have a chip on your shoulder about the Theater Department." He paused again, studying her. Amanda hoped her face was remaining opaque. "So my guess is, there was someone—" His face darkened suddenly. "Say, you weren't involved with that Collins character, were you?"

She'd been tensing up, but the image of the roly-poly professor as her past paramour was so absurd she laughed. "Professor Collins isn't my type," she told him.

Ethan appeared relieved. "I didn't think so."

"But you'd make a decent detective," she admitted.

"There was a man, an actor named Brad Sonders. And yes, we were involved, at Deermount... and he left, and I didn't," she finished abruptly, still finding the subject too difficult to talk about objectively.

"But it wasn't that simple, was it?" Ethan's voice was soft, sympathetic. "I'm sorry, I didn't mean to probe too deeply into a sensitive area."

She felt the open friendliness emanating from his concerned eyes. Perhaps it was the wine, the candlelight, or the sincerity in his words, but she felt for the first time that she might be able to trust him.

"It's all right," she said. "I shouldn't be so sensitive about it at this late date." She shrugged. "When I met Brad, some five years ago, he was playing his first role at the amphiteater: Mercutio, in *Romeo and Juliet*. He was gorgeous, dashing..." She sighed ruefully. "To this day I'm not sure whether I fell in love with him or the character he played."

"That's something actors get confused about themselves."

"I know." She nodded, and sipped her wine. "He was younger than me—a sophomore, and I was a senior. I'd been considering staying on at Deermount to do some graduate work, and hooking up with Brad clinched it. They had a three-year program, so the timing seemed good. We moved in together during his junior year. We played house in a little place off campus, and we got engaged in the summer."

"Sounds idyllic. What went wrong?"

For a fleeting moment Amanda wondered why she was telling him all this, but she plunged on, feeling that his interest was genuine. "Well, we weren't the most ideal match to begin with... and we started growing apart, even as we lived together. The more Brad got absorbed in his work, the bigger his ego seemed to expand—and the less time he had for me. You know, it's funny; you'd think that two people living under the same roof would spend a lot of time together. We ended up seeing each other less than we had before."

Ethan nodded. "I'm familiar with that syndrome," he commented. "Go on."

"Well, the plan had been to marry after Brad's graduation. But by the time the end of his last semester rolled around, we were barely friends—or lovers. He'd just become so full of himself!" She shook her head, the memories still incensing her. "He never took *my* work or *my* ambitions seriously... and the difference in our ages suddenly seemed to mean more than it had. When we met, I thought he was mature for his age. But as time went on, his inexperience..." She let the words trail off, suddenly embarrassed. There were some details about their relationship she didn't feel like sharing with a stranger, even a friendly one. Certainly the specifics of her love life with Brad could be omitted.

"An older man would suit you better."

She looked at Ethan quickly, but his face showed no self-promoting smirk. "Maybe so," she said dryly. "At any rate, the topper came when he got an offer to go to Los Angeles. I had a year left before I'd get my Ph.D., and when push came to shove, he couldn't wait around. Hollywood called, and the wedding bells got stifled—for good."

She saw the empathy in his warm gaze and felt the force of his compassion for her unspoken hurt. Too much wine on an empty stomach, she told herself, that must account for the flock of butterflies in my gut.

"You must have been disappointed," he said.

"Oh, I don't blame Brad. It's just as well things worked

out that way—for both of us. He's moved into the movies, and I'm establishing my own career, right here."

"Any man who would leave you for a screen test has scrambled priorities to say the least," he said. "I guess the world is full of more fools than I thought."

"Doesn't your work come first?" A tingling awareness that his hand was now covering hers made casual banter difficult, but she was doing her best to seem unaffected.

"Often enough, I guess." His voice lowered as his eyes once more intently studied her face. "But right now wild horses couldn't tear me away..."

As he leaned forward, a plate of hot cornbread materialized between them. Amanda took the opportunity to remove her hand. Freed from the magnetic spell of his gaze, she realized she was ravenously hungry.

"Dig in," said Ethan as the waitress brought her chicken over. She was happy to, aware that she'd talked a lot about herself, which wasn't in the plan. She tried to remember she was supposed to be on her guard. The man's engaging friendliness was making that difficult.

All conversation was briefly suspended, though, as they began to eat. The chicken had a special tangy sauce with some secret spice that literally made her mouth water. The vegetables were fresh and cooked to perfection.

As they finished off one bottle of wine and began another, Ethan questioned her about her work. Amanda soon discovered to her chagrin that he was far from unschooled. The playwright knew as much, if not more, about classic literature and drama than many of her colleagues. He was as impassioned in his opinions as she was and delighted by a good, full-tilt intellectual brawl.

"Wordsworth?" He put his knife down with a resounding clatter. "Would you like to look up the word 'humbug' in the dictionary? They have his picture next to it."

Amanda laughed. She was so used to the pedantic, flowery discourses of her fellow faculty members that Ethan's lively insights, unfettered by rhetoric, were a welcome breath of fresh air. "At least he was grammatical," she sallied. "At least he didn't rely on four-letter words for effect."

"Well, neither does Albee, or Pinter, or anyone else who's writing serious drama these days. Scaring the audience with scatological language went out with incense and lovebeads. Say, you can use your fingers," he added as Amanda wrestled with a particularly problematic piece of chicken. "It's fine with me, and I'm sure Molly herself would encourage you."

Amanda lifted the chicken wing in as ladylike a manner as possible. Ethan beamed at her, his face flushed with the wine and enthusiasm for their friendly argument. No longer self-conscious beneath his appreciative gaze, she ate the last choice morsels, feeling giddy and bold.

"Don't get me wrong," Ethan was saying, watching her carefully dry her sauce-covered fingertips with her napkin. "I like a strong form and structure. But it's what you've got to say that makes a poem or a play meaningful."

"Truce!" she smiled. "I'll withhold judgment until I see the latest Broadway has to offer."

"Maybe my new play will convince you."

"Convince me what?"

"That the theater isn't dead. That dramatic poetry didn't end with Restoration drama."

"I doubt I'll get to see it."

"I doubt I'll let you miss it." He took hold of her wrist with one hand, looking into her eyes, and gently pulled her hand toward his lips.

The warm wetness of his brief, intimate caress seemed to penetrate her skin and travel the length of her arm to course through her entire body. She was conscious of a now-familiar tingling in her stomach, but she was somehow unable to pull her hand away. He held it, still gazing at her, that gentle glow radiating from his dark eyes. Focus! she commanded herself. He's melting down your last defenses.

"But I'll be here," she said. "Where I belong," With an extreme exertion of will power, she slipped her hand from his. "And you'll be—"

"I may be back before long," he said, frowning. "Despite your persistent objections. Actually, there is more involved in my wanting to be in Ohio than the residency offer." He paused. Amanda was reminded again of how careful Ethan was about revealing himself. "My Dad lives on a farm not far from here," he said slowly, as if reluctant to impart this information. "He's getting on in years. I figure if I've got a chance to spend some time with him next summer, I should grab the opportunity."

"You grew up in Ohio?"

"No, Massachusetts. The old man moved out here some ten years ago, when my Mom passed away. It's where he was born."

"You come from a big family?" She was determined to draw him out.

"Just one sister."

"Older?"

"Younger." He smiled. "You're asking a lot of questions."

"You've been doing most of the asking. I'm only trying to even the balance."

"I see." He nodded. "I'm sorry if I was a little close-lipped this morning. I guess I've become overprotective about my private life. Why, it's gotten to the point where I don't even introduce myself to people I pull out of rivers."

"If you're seeking to avoid publicity, then you've come to the wrong place," Amanda pointed out. "Half the student body's going to follow you around if you teach here."

Ethan sighed. "You don't give up easily, do you?" He leaned back, looking at her through narrowed eyes. "I don't mind a drama student who wants to learn something about the craft asking me questions. It's the media that I despise—the press."

"Why?" She was reminded of Deborah Varrone. Though the undeniable enjoyment of Ethan's company had kept the spectre of Sono Araki from floating to the forefront of her mind, suddenly it was there for her to confront. "What have you got to hide?" she blurted out.

Ethan's brow darkened. "I like to think my work speaks for itself," he said quietly. "I've had my psyche dissected in the Sunday papers for the public's perusal; I've had things read into my work you wouldn't believe, but that's only to be expected—critics are an imaginative breed. What I do resent is the media's perverse greed for the intimate details of my personal life, real or invented."

Amanda looked up, watching him closely, hoping he would continue.

"Sometimes when the press can't dig up some sordid dirt that'll make a catchy headline, they'll plant something, true or not, just to increase circulation. It's happened to me. At the time I was most vulnerable, the press behaved shamelessly." Ethan seemed momentarily lost in somber contemplation. Then, as though he had shaken off whatever memory was disturbing him, he looked up, meeting Amanda's curious gaze. "I do go on, don't I?" he said in a lighter tone. "I'll bet you're sorry you asked."

"No, I . . ." She wasn't. Had the press distorted the truth about his wife's death? The thought was oddly reassuring. But as much as she was curious to know more, she realized that Ethan's personal tragedy was not the sort of subject to bandy about between glasses of wine. She regretted casting a pall over the conversation. "I agree with you," she said. "Writers have a right to their privacy. Any artist does."

He smiled. "Don't tell me you might consider what I do for a living to be art," he said with mock surprise.

"Let's say the jury's still out."

His smile was contagious. His hand covered hers again, and her skin pulsed to life. Once more, his eyes pulled her into their warm, dark depths.

"Well, now that I've overcome at least some of your prejudices, and we've finished our second bottle of wine," he said, "I think there's only one thing left for us to do."

A number of deliciously wicked thoughts swirled through Amanda's mind. She shook them off. "What's that?" she asked, affecting nonchalance as her pulse raced at his touch.

"Let's dance."

"Here? Now?"

"Sure," he said, pulling her up with him as he rose from the table. "It's the 'Tennessee Waltz.'"

As if that were reason enough! Her heart pounded as she faced him, her palm moist in his grip. She felt a flare of rebellion. This man who stomped around Broadway in cowboy boots was already assuming that his charismatic charm had won him another conquest. She tried to pull away, but his gentle grip became firmer. His eyes glinted mischievously. He seemed to relish her defiance.

"No one's watching," he said. It was a challenge.

Her quick glance at the bar confirmed that its few inhabitants seemed solely interested in their beers. She looked back at Ethan. "I don't care if they do," she said, a surge of recklessness overtaking her better judgment. He smiled. Then his arm slid around her waist, and he swept her out to the center of the floor.

The country music was sweetly haunting in her ears as he placed his hand on her bare shoulder. His body pressed against hers. She shivered, inhaling his clean, masculine scent, which reminded her of evergreens. The fingers of his right hand intertwined with hers, and his left slid slowly down from her shoulder to rest against the small of her back. She could feel Ethan's heart beating, felt the subtle shift in her own heartbeat as it joined his.

They were dancing in a slow, swaying rhythm, at one with each other and the even, lazy beat of the jukebox tune. Amanda was aroused by how perfectly her body seemed to mold to his, how effortlessly they turned together, circling the sawdust-covered space beyond the tables.

"You'd think we'd done this before," Ethan whispered close to her ear as if reading her thoughts aloud. His fingers glided slowly up and down her spine. He held her even closer. She was conscious of his pelvis moving against hers and her own hips swaying, interlocking with his, an exquisite warmth simmering up from the depths of her loins. His lips brushed her cheek briefly as she turned her head, feeling dizzy. She closed her eyes, an involuntary sigh of pleasure escaping her lips.

You're supposed to be giving him second thoughts about next summer, she thought hazily. What happened to your second thoughts about tonight?

But any thoughts at all were being overridden by the power of his arms around her, his lips nuzzling the tip of her ear, his soft hand on her skin.

For a moment she could barely breathe. She lifted her face, forcing her eyes open. Their faces were only inches apart. She was staring into his dark eyes, seeing her own reflection amidst the flecks of gold. She parted her lips, and the air she breathed in was mingled with his breath. She couldn't will her lips to close. The warm strength of his body pressed hard against hers was sending ripples of liquid sensation through her.

His first kiss was soft, a gentle brushing of his lips across hers. But then those lips were pressing more forcefully, the soft tip of his tongue parting them wider, and it was as though her lips had caught fire. Her tongue sought his, as if to quench the flame, but it only burned hotter, like a fever running through her veins. Their tongues circled in an inner dance as their feet slowed. She was dimly aware of the music fading. Her heart was pounding madly as at last she pulled away.

The music had ended, and the dance should have been over, but she was still in Ethan's arms. His eyes held hers, a shine in them she'd never seen before, so bright it was almost scary.

"I've never met a professor who danced as well as you do," he said.

"You mean the other professors you've danced with were all left feet?"

Ethan smiled. "Song's over," he said.

But neither of them moved. Amanda looked at him,

feeling abnormally light-headed, waiting for her pulse to slow down and for the room to sit still. She'd imagined that it had kept spinning around them when they'd stopped dancing. Ethan looked suddenly to their right, and she followed his gaze. Three men were sitting at the bar, staring at the two of them as expectantly as baseball fans waiting for the next pitch.

Ethan quietly cleared his throat. The three heads turned back to their beers.

"I could use some fresh air," said Amanda. Maybe oxygen would revive her rationality. She was getting completely carried away.

"There's a garden in the back," he said.

He guided her through the door off the entrance to the kitchen. She found herself in a little grove that was filled with the scent of hyacinth and the chirp of a vast cricket orchestra. Molly's place was on a rise. The hill Amanda stood on banked down, rolling to vast open meadows she could dimly make out, a patchwork of deep gray-greens. She could see the outlines of tree tops below them, softly swaying in the evening breeze. The moon above was like a bright white pearl set in a sky of black velvet, netted with the gossamer strands of twinkling silver stars.

She felt Ethan behind her. She meant to move away, but his arms slid around her waist. How could she resist being molded to his sinewy body, or reject the soft, feathery kisses his lips rained on her arching neck? As his tongue tickled a shiver-provoking trail from her earlobe to her collarbone, a soft moan escaped her lips.

"Such soft skin . . ." he whispered, " . . . as sweet as milk and honey . . ." Ethan's hands moved slowly up her taut stomach to cup the quivering mounds of her breasts. His fingertips made a slow, circular motion around their swelling tips, which strained against the soft lace of the bra encasing them. Nothing in her experience had prepared her for the molten fire that ran through her veins at his caress. As he continued to kiss the silky nape of her neck, the flesh beneath his gently kneading fingers threatened to burn through the material. An aching desire to press herself against him, to feel all his hard length, overcame her. Amanda turned in the circle of his arms to face Ethan. She kissed him hungrily with a sudden, passionate fierceness.

His lips answered her in kind, covering hers with devouring intensity, his tongue searching, driving hard into her mouth. Her tongue melted against his. She moved restlessly against him, arching her back in the grip of his powerful embrace, feeling the rise and fall of his muscular chest against her heaving breasts.

His fingers tenderly stroked her fevered cheeks, then twisted the curls of hair about her ears. He broke abruptly from their kiss. He cupped her chin in the crook of his thumb and forefinger, his eyes drinking in the wild abandonment that she felt must have been shining from her face.

"Let me look at you." His voice was a husky rasp of desire. "You were made for moonlight," he whispered. "Or was moonlight made for you?"

The last vestiges of rational thought evaporated.

As Ethan ran his hands through the shimmering tresses of her hair, she could only think of wanting him, wanting him with a desire that was nearly painful.

He could take me here and now, and I'd surrender, she thought, dimly shocked at the wicked excitement the idea aroused in her.

"I came out here to get some air," she said, weak beneath the smoldering beams of his eyes, "but I still can't seem to catch my breath. Maybe we'd better go back in."

"What would you say," he began, not letting go of her, gently running the tip of one finger along the curve of her lower lip, "to a moonlit ride through those open fields down there...and maybe a stroll through a meadow...with a jug of wine and me?"

"I'd say you were plagiarizing, badly," she said, and took a playful bite at his finger before he pulled it away. "No loaf of bread?"

"After Molly's cooking?" He cocked his head, listening. The soft strains of a pedal steel guitar wafted through the tavern's open window. "They're playing our song again...and I believe we're alone, this time. Miss Farr?"

Wordlessly, she fell into the circle of his strong arms. As they began to sway slowly together to the muffled, sweetly mournful music, Amanda rested her head on Ethan's shoulder. The wind picked up, sending a cascade of her long hair over his arm. She trembled suddenly, more with an exquisite mixture of desire and anticipation than with the cold.

"Amanda," he sighed, and his soft voice by her ear sounded sweet as a mockingbird's call. "What a perfect fit you are—"

"Ethan? Ethan...is that you?"

The unfamiliar voice that broke Amanda's reverie was like a splash of icy water on her brow. She felt Ethan stiffen at the sound. Amanda pulled away from him as a woman silhouetted in the light of the doorway approached them.

Chapter
4

"I FIGURED I'D find you here. I'm sorry, Ethan, but I just had to come get you."

The woman, Amanda saw, had red hair and a comely figure in tight, worn blue jeans and a man's tailored denim shirt. Bewildered, Amanda watched as Ethan walked quickly to meet her, then held a low-voiced conference with her by the doorway. The redhead made animated gestures as Ethan nodded slowly, hands on his hips, lips set tight, obviously displeased by what she had to say.

Amanda didn't know which was more humiliating: her embarrassment at the sudden, unwelcome intrusion, or the keen, burning edge to the resentment she was feeling toward the intruder that to her chagrin she recognized as jealousy.

Then Ethan was walking back over to her, a scowl on his face. The red-haired woman hovered in the doorway, looking after him, then disappeared inside the tavern.

"Amanda, I've got a little problem—"

"Little? Well, she is shorter than you, that's true," she snapped, wondering at her own hostility.

Ethan shot her a puzzled look. "Kristin? No, honey, that's my sister. The problem is my production in New York—"

"Your sister?"

Ethan sighed. "That's right. Kristin's out here visiting Dad, just as I am. He's not feeling too well." He waited to see the flames simmer down in Amanda's eyes, then went on: "Casey Roberts just walked out on our show—the director. I guess he got tired of these producers trying to butt in on every rehearsal. I should have seen this coming," he said more to himself. "Anyway, I've got to talk to him, quick, and see if we can pull things back together. Damn show's supposed to open in less than ten days."

"That sounds terrible, Ethan," she said, sensing his agitation from the tenseness she saw in his face.

"I think I can work it out. Casey's an old friend. But that's not the only thing." He looked at her, his face showing a different kind of concern now. "My flight leaves in an hour and a half."

"Tonight?" She hadn't meant the word to squeak, but she felt as if her stomach had just plummeted a few feet.

"Tonight," he said sadly, pushing a strand of hair from her eye.

Crushed, maddened by the unfairness of fate, and feeling more frustration than she'd felt in years, Amanda feigned a good-natured, cavalier attitude on the drive back to Silver Falls. Nevertheless she couldn't help feeling irrationally indignant. Once again, theater had wreaked havoc with her romantic life. It conjured up bad, Brad-related associations.

"I nearly missed my own wedding night after it got postponed twice—an opening night shifted dates," Ethan was saying with a rueful chuckle. Did he sense her annoyance? Amanda watched fence posts caught in the headlight's beams fly by, wondering what kind of a woman Sono Araki had been. She wondered how people in the theater sustained their relationships when this kind of abrupt coming and going seemed to be the norm.

Then the Thunderbird was pulling into her driveway. Ethan insisted on walking her up the stairs to her door. As she stood on the landing, looking for her keys, she wanted to believe that the worried look on his face arose out of sincere concern for her feelings. But perhaps his mind was on New York City and the conflicts he'd have to deal with as soon as his plane touched ground.

"I'm sorry our time got cut short," he said softly.

"That's show biz," she said with false brightness.

He smiled and, before she could turn her key in the door, had pressed his lips softly against her forehead.

"Now listen, Professor," he said, halting her with a hand on her shoulder. "Don't disappear on me. Because I'll be back. I want to pick things up right where we left them—as soon as possible." He drew her to him. The force of their embrace wrenched all her stifled feelings loose. Feeling his warm, strong body against hers, she was nearly overcome by a combination of bittersweet disappointment and frustrated anger.

Then he was gone, bounding down the stairs to his car. Amanda didn't wait to watch him drive off but hurried inside. He'd said wild horses couldn't tear him away. Obviously dissatisfied directors could. Theater people! She should have known better.

She couldn't wait for this unbelievably long Friday to end. She yearned for the solace of a good night's sleep.

For about two minutes, when some shampoo got in her eye while she attempted to wash that man right out of her hair, Amanda succeeded in not thinking about Ethan Taylor. But the rest of the morning was a case of trying not to think about a pink elephant: Big rosy trunks and floppy ears were everywhere she looked.

She began cleaning her room, usually a distracting task. She ended up standing frozen by the bed with the dress she'd worn last night in her hands, smelling phantom hyacinth and reliving moonlit caresses. When she considered taking a stroll in the Glen, she was immediately transported to the river bank by the little bridge, remembering those eyes... Short of hitting herself over the head with a blunt instrument, what could she do with herself that would banish all thoughts of Ethan Taylor from her mind?

Well, she did have a symposium on Chaucer to develop. She could spend the afternoon doing research. Feeling more centered now that she had a plan, Amanda got into some jeans and her favorite sweater—an oversized pink angora—threw on a jacket, and set out for the campus bookstore.

Shocking yellow leaves spattered with scarlet flurried in the air around her, then flew off. The bright sunlight and the clean, woodsy air invigorated her. By the time she'd reached campus, Amanda felt clear-headed enough to venture a quick, clinical check on her emotional state. How *did* she feel about last night, really?

She was angry—and ecstatic. She was bitterly disappointed at how things had turned out—and genuinely relieved. She yearned to see Ethan Taylor again—and fervently hoped he was out of her life for good.

"Well," she muttered aloud, "it's good to know I'm not the least bit ambivalent."

"Excuse me?"

The brown-haired student in jogging sweats standing next to her on the corner shot her a quizzical look. Amanda bit her lower lip in embarrassment and shook her head, indicating he should pay her no mind. He grinned, and trotted off as the stop light on Spring Street changed to green.

Great, Amanda mused, one day and a night with Ethan Taylor and I'm talking to myself on the street.

Go engross yourself in a good book, she commanded herself sternly, thinking of the avenue of escape from painful emotions that she'd resorted to since childhood. Accordingly, she headed for the book store, the Silver Serif, which was just around the corner. Soon she was scanning its shelves for a volume of literary criticism on fourteenth-century prose that she had meant to buy for sometime. Curling up in bed with it would be a welcome treat.

It wasn't her fault that the literature section of the Silver Serif ended at the beginning of Drama. And could she be blamed for the prominently displayed stack of brightly bound hardcover books bearing the title *Ethan Taylor: Collected Plays* directly to her right? It was only natural that the book's bold colors would claim her attention. Any person in her position, Amanda assured herself, would pick up a copy of the book and, with a look of mild curiosity, briefly scan its contents.

Then, feeling much like a devious teenager who furtively flips to the centerfold of a man's magazine filched from a candy-store rack, Amanda quickly turned to the black-and-white photo pages in the middle of the thick book. Most of the photos, stills from various productions of Ethan's plays, were of little interest for the moment. She found what she was looking for on the last page of the section.

The slight overexposure from the flashbulb's glare did nothing to diminish the striking, exotic beauty of the woman sitting next to Ethan in this more candid shot, taken, its caption informed her, "At a rehearsal for *Liberty's Last Dance:* Ethan Taylor with his wife, famed designer Sono Araki." Sono's hair was cut stylishly short in a fashion that distinctively framed the pale, perfect complexion of her oval face. Her features were small, delicate: her slightly hooded eyes and doll-like lips as exquisite as the deft brush strokes of an Oriental master calligrapher. Amanda hated the sight of her with a passion she found alarming.

Sono wasn't facing the photographer, but rather looking at Ethan with an expression Amanda could only describe as proprietary. He's *mine,* she seemed to say with her eyes. Ethan had his arm draped casually around Sono's shoulders. He leaned back in his chair, staring at the camera, his eyes telegraphing his displeasure at having to sit still for such foolishness.

Amanda turned to the back of the book. The biographical information was so sketchy that she assumed it was the product of Ethan's deliberate smokescreening. The short paragraph did, at least, give his date of birth. A quick calculation told her he was thirty-six, eight years older than she. He'd attended Bard, the small but prestigious liberal arts college in the Northeast. He'd started winning awards within a year or two of his first production, and in the midst of piling up the bigger prizes had married Sono Araki when he was twenty-six. There was no mention of children, Amanda noted thankfully. When she realized that this fact had made her feel better, she slammed the book shut and returned it to its shelf.

After circling the Serif in search of *The Fourteenth Century: A History in Prose* and finding herself instead in front of Ethan's book for the third consecutive time, she finally bought the damn thing, shelling out what she felt was an exorbitant figure for such dubiously commercial writing. The critical volume she still hadn't managed to locate would have been half the price.

The book lay in its paper bag on Amanda's desk for most of the weekend. She regarded it from a safe distance, as if it were a present from persons unknown that conceivably could be booby-trapped.

Saturday night she went out with Claudia Renfield. Fashion model-thin, with a wild and woolly head of curly brown hair, Claudia was Deermount's painter-in-residence art teacher and Amanda's closest friend on campus. After a silly but diverting Peter Sellers comedy at the Campus Collective Cinema, the two women had a light bite at Montana's, a bar and grill down the street. Amanda felt she was recovering her equilibrium. Since Claudia was always urging her to date more and was bound to deluge her with questions, Amanda avoided going into details about her meeting Ethan Taylor.

"He's a fantastic-looking guy," commented Claudia, studying Amanda's face. "You like him?"

"He's a good dancer," she admitted.

"You danced? With him?" Claudia shook her head. "This sounds like something serious."

"Not at all," she scoffed, and she met her friend's inquisitive stare with a heavily edited version of her date with Ethan that made the experience seem more like an amusing literary anecdote. Making light of the encounter distanced her from it, took the emotional charge out of it. But later, lying alone in what suddenly seemed an all-too-quiet apartment, she still felt so charged she was surprised she wasn't glowing in the dark. She regretted not having confided more in Claudia and gotten her true feelings out in the open.

By Sunday afternoon she considered the telephone to

be a malevolent being. It hadn't rung. But she told herself this was just as well. Under a large weeping willow in a secluded corner of the Glen, she opened Ethan's book, determined to dislike and discredit every word the man had written.

To begin with, the titles of his plays were preposterous: *The Junkie Saints. Gunslinger's Heart. Dog Star and the Moonbeams.* They sounded more like the names of rock'n'roll bands than works of weighty dramaturgy. His characters had equally outrageous names, like Jughead, Tooth, and Cantina. It was as if the man were defying one to take him seriously. Maybe his prize-winner would clue her in to what the fuss was all about. She began to read *Cry of the Dakota Angels.*

There was no question that Ethan Taylor could write. He wrote so movingly, powerfully, that she had to admit the awards and accolades seemed to have been well-earned. His style was a heady, gutsy mixture of street-wise dialogue that blossomed into lyrical poetry. His vividly drawn characters strove to be heroic in a world where ideals rarely survived. An hour and a half later, Amanda found the play's final lines blurring beneath her gaze. It was because her eyes were full of tears.

If reading the play had devastated her, she could imagine its effect when performed live on stage. No wonder he was championed by critics and laymen alike. He broke every rule that Amanda had studied and taught, taking courageous risks, and he succeeded. She should have found his writing offensive. Instead, she found it brilliant.

By sundown she'd devoured two more plays and was hungry for more. By midnight she'd had her fill of the written word. Tossing and turning in a bed that had grown painfully empty, she wanted Ethan Taylor in the flesh. She could still feel the feathery touch of his lips on her throat...

Monday morning the telephone was shrilly ringing when she reentered the house with milk and the morning paper. She nearly did herself grave bodily harm by vaulting over her bed at breakneck speed to reach it. But the voice that answered her breathless hello was female. It was Sherman McGuinness's secretary, confirming the poet's arrival time at the Dayton airport for four-fifteen that day and checking on his accommodations in Silver Falls.

Amanda assured the woman that the nicest room the Silver Falls Inn had to offer had been booked, noting that McGuinness seemed to be on the fussy side. This was the third such phone call she'd received in the past week, going over the same ground. Then, with a deep breath and crossed fingers, Amanda inquired if the poet might be free for dinner that evening, as she'd like to introduce herself and acquaint him with his itinerary for the following day.

The secretary put her on hold. A moment later, she was informed that dinner at the inn at half past seven would be of the utmost satisfaction to Mr. McGuinness.

Striding briskly to her office, Amanda felt a renewed surge of well-being. She'd been looking forward to this meeting for a long time. And hopefully, it would help lift her out of what was turning into a deep depression.

At first she'd been almost relieved she hadn't heard from Ethan Taylor. But now the lack of communication from him maddened her. Whatever trust she'd begun to have in the man was rapidly evaporating. Certainly he was busy, but three mornings had passed with no word. She was starting to think that their night together had been a casual flirtation for him, after all. The thought made her blood boil. Well, she could be casual, too. She decided she was best off putting their abortive almost-fling behind her. Chapter closed.

It was a good idea, but its execution was difficult when half the students on campus carried copies of Ethan's play collection. Word was evidently out that the celebrity had been on campus and might be returning. Amanda was glad that no one, student or teacher, had seen them together. Their meetings had been clandestine, and she considered that fortuitous: She didn't want to be quizzed on the playwright's favorite color or become a piece of gossip herself.

At seven-twenty-eight, she stood in the lobby of the inn wearing one of her favorite dresses, a clingy turquoise crepe that left her shoulders bare and picked up the color of her eyes. Precisely two minutes later, Sherman McGuinness descended the staircase. He was immaculate in a dark, conservatively cut suit, thin as a rail, graying at the temples—and about as stiff in his bearing as a knight carved in marble.

"Delighted to make your acquaintance," he said in a dry, sandpapery voice, smiling with evident satisfaction at her appearance. He held her hand a beat too long as she introduced herself. His eyes inspected her with uncomfortable intensity as they walked to the restaurant's entrance across the lobby.

Amanda had never eaten at the Silver Falls Inn because besides being expensive, its atmosphere was stodgy and old-fashioned, catering as it did to visiting parents and alumni. Sherman McGuinness seemed completely at home. Within minutes of their being seated, Amanda began to get a sinking feeling that McGuinness in person was not going to live up to McGuinness in print.

"One sees so many of these little towns when one is on a tour," he said. "I suppose there's some quaint bookshop that will request autographing from me, there always is—not that I'll have time, mind you—I'm off to Seattle late tomorrow night to accept some sort of honorarium...Tell me," he said suddenly, leaning forward. "What *is* that perfume you have on? It's positively ambrosial!"

Ambrosial! The waitress had arrived, momentarily sparing Amanda the poet's attentions. As the meal progressed, McGuinness proceeded to make a nervous wreck of the waitress, with a dozen condescending harassments. His conversation, Amanda noted, seemed to consist almost entirely of sentences beginning with "I." In between pompous pronouncements on the nature of good poetry (his own) and bad (anyone else's), he openly ogled her body, attempting physical contact with her whenever he could manage it and showing not the slightest interest in anything she said.

"I'm always seeking beauty in the most wayward places—it is a poet's chosen crusade, I suppose—and I'm most gratified to have you end my quest, Miss Farr, so quickly, on my first night in Silver Falls."

"You're too kind." She fidgeted in her seat, removing her hand that McGuinness had trapped beneath his. As they drank their coffee "a pitifully undistinguished blend," McGuinnes noted, Amanda found memories of her dinner with Ethan floating through her mind. Suddenly the absent playwright seemed very attractive. Though in physical appearance McGuinness was closer to her image of a famous author, in fact, her idol was an obnoxious old bore.

One important thing had been accomplished, though. McGuinness was interested, logically enough, in reading the rough draft of her study of him. Amanda doubted she'd have trouble securing his approval of her work. The only difficulty, she surmised, would be keeping McGuinness at arm's length. She narrowly avoided his intended kiss goodnight by executing a deft, Houdini-esque maneuver that left him holding her hand. Then she was rid of her clay-footed idol.

Having reached the conclusion that the only good author was a dead one, Amanda curled up in bed with a tattered copy of *Alice in Wonderland*. It was secretly her favorite book, and one refreshingly devoid of too much literary significance. Not long after Alice began to swim in a pool of her own tears, Amanda began to feel weepy herself. She put the book aside, turned out the light, and snuffled into her pillow for a few minutes. Then, deciding she was too old to be feeling or acting like this, she sat up in bed. She wondered if that bottle of brandy she'd been given as a gift once was still stuck in the back of a kitchen cabinet.

The phone rang.

She stared at it in disbelief, checked the clock, noting it was after midnight, let three rings pass, then picked it up.

"Professor? Did I wake you?"

Even long distance, Ethan's husky, musical drawl made her ear vibrate with a sensual tingle. She tried not to let her excitement show as she answered, "Wake me? No, I was actually on my way out. Monday nights, the discotheques in Silver Falls don't start jumping until after midnight."

He chuckled. "Can you hang on long enough to listen to an apology?"

"I suppose. Just this once."

"Amanda, for the past forty-eight hours I haven't spoken to anyone but my typewriter. Rewriting was the only way to solve the particular problems Carey and I've been having with the producers. I would've called sooner, but honestly, it's been impossible." He paused. "You still with me?"

"I'm listening," she said. She was also smiling like a happy idiot, as she could see in the mirror over the bureau opposite her bed. Cool down, Amanda, she warned her reflection. The man could be handing you one of his well-crafted lines.

"I had this crazy idea you might think I wasn't being sincere about the other night," he said.

"About what?"

"About my intention to pick things up right where we had to leave them." The memory of his hands gliding around her in the moonlight quickened her breathing. "Well, I know that it's a little late, but this is my earliest opportunity to tell you—I'm on my way back to do just that."

Her lips were dry. She wet them with her tongue. "Really?" she said. "I'll try to save a little space for you sometime before the New Year."

"I plan on being there a lot sooner than that."

"Take your time, Mr. Taylor," she told him.

"When I get there, Miss Farr, I certainly intend to."

She could picture the impish grin behind his playful words. Her heart beat faster. She was suddenly unable to act cool, calm, and collected.

"Ethan, are you really coming back to—" she began to ask, but he interrupted suddenly, asking her to hold on. Amanda could hear a muffled female voice on the other end of the line, cajoling Ethan to get off the phone. Then he was back, sounding harried.

"Amanda, I've got to run. I'm sorry to be so brief—"

"It's par for the course," she said dryly. "Got company?"

"Company?" He sounded puzzled. Then he laughed. "Oh, yes. I'm up to my neck in dancing girls here. Seriously, Amanda, I'm needed, I'm afraid—"

"I won't keep you," she said. "Drop me a line sometime."

She hung up. Whether or not Ethan had actually been with another woman was none of her business, and of course she believed him anyway. Didn't she? Amanda sighed. At least he had called. And he said he was coming back. Should she believe that? Amanda lay back on the bed. One thing was certain: Sleep was still a long way off.

Chapter 5

AT FIRST SHE thought the sound that had awakened her was tree branches scraping against the window by her bed. She reached over and raised the shade, blearily examining the spindly white arms of the birches trembling in the wind. They didn't appear to be the source. Her alarm had yet to go off, she saw in the early morning light. Maybe she'd imagined—

There it was again: a rattling sound, something hitting the panes, like hail or...stones? Stones being thrown up at her window? Amanda lifted the shade again, looked outside, then quickly lowered it. No. She was either still asleep or hallucinating. Ethan Taylor was in New York.

When she let go of the shade, it snapped out of her hand and rolled up to the top of the window with a violent clatter, suddenly flooding the room with sunlight. She cowered on the bed for a moment, shocked into wide-awakeness, then ventured another look out the window. There was indeed a blue Thunderbird parked in her driveway.

Amanda climbed out of bed, threw her white terry-cloth robe over the old-fashioned cotton nightgown she had on, and strode barefooted to the kitchen door. He must have sprinted up the flight of stairs that ran along the side of the garage, because he was already standing expectantly on the landing outside when she unlocked the door and opened it.

"Good morning," said Ethan Taylor, thumbs looped in the waistband of his tight brown corduroys, a breeze ruffling his hair, his eyes gleaming in the warm rust morning light. She tried to ignore the tiny tremors of arousal she felt as his admiring gaze swept fleetingly over her face and lingered on the pale skin revealed at the open neck of her robe.

"You know," he said, "I've seen you drenched to the bone, I've seen you all dressed up, I've seen you now fresh out of bed—and you always look incredible. How do you account for that, Professor?"

"Flattery just might get you a cup of coffee," she said. "Come on in."

She held the door open for him, stiffening as his body brushed hers in passing. As Amanda watched him saunter into her kitchen, she decided that Ethan Taylor was the only man she'd ever met who emanated a magnetic field.

"I don't mean to pry," she said, shutting the door behind him, "but aren't you in the middle of a rehearsal?"

"Had to take a break," he said. She watched him examine the kitchen furnishings she'd carefully assembled over the years: a white- and black-trim art deco table from New Orleans she'd unearthed in a garage sale, two black-topped chrome stools that had once resided at Lou's Drugstore fountain counter in town, and some framed antique magazine covers adorning the pale rose walls. Ethan nodded to himself, as if it all added up to something he understood. "I like your taste in Americana," was his laconic comment.

"These old things?" she joked. "Thanks." Keeping as wide a distance from him as possible, she went to the stove and lit the gas flame beneath the kettle. As she stepped to the counter to fetch some coffee, he was suddenly in front of her. His hands gently but firmly grasped her shoulders, stopping her in mid-stride.

"Now, where were we?" he murmured.

"En route to coffee," she said, her heart beating loudly in her ears. His face slowly came closer to hers. Even as she opened her mouth to protest, he was ever-so-lightly brushing his lips across the tip of her nose. "Ethan—" she began, as a shudder coursed through her at his touch.

Her alarm went off.

"Excuse me," she muttered, breaking away. Amanda went into the bedroom and quickly quieted the buzzing clock. When she returned to the kitchen, she paused by the doorway. If she could keep a few feet between them, maybe she could fight off the crazy temptation she'd just had to melt inside the shelter of Ethan's arms.

"I hope you don't mind a quick cup of coffee," she told him. "I have a class to teach in forty minutes."

"You mean I flew six-hundred miles in the dead of night," he said with raised eyebrows, "for a quick cup of coffee?"

"Ethan, do you expect me to believe that you came back here just to see me?"

"Yes," he said with a smile, and sat down at the kitchen table. "Even though it'll also be nice to see my Dad."

"Is he all right?"

Ethan frowned. "Well, I'd checked in with Kristin just before I spoke to you last night. It seems his lumbago is giving him an unusually hard time." He paused as Amanda turned the flame off under the whistling kettle. "I peeked in on him just now, before I drove over. He's sleeping, which is a good sign."

Amanda shook some ground coffee from a jar into a filter. "You really care about your father, don't you?"

"I love him," he said simply. She felt his eyes watching her as she poured hot water over the grounds. "But you're the real reason for my being here." He looked at her briefly, then lowered his eyes. "You sounded pretty skeptical on the phone last night. I thought I ought to make it out here and tell you in person. That . . . that I can't seem to sleep at night. That your face floats into my dreams. That . . . that I miss you . . ."

"You don't have to tell me such things," she said. "The coffee's ready." She put a steaming cup in front of him. "Milk and sugar?"

He shook his head. "You don't believe me?"

Amanda sighed. "At this hour of the morning, compliments tend to bring out the cynic in me." She turned back to the counter and poured a cup for herself.

"Cynic? That's not a word I'd use in describing you," he said. "Actually, you've reaffirmed my belief in the existense of earthly angels."

She sensed him getting up behind her. Her body tensed as his arms slid around her waist, and she felt his warm breath at her ear.

"Why are you trying so hard to mistrust me?" he whispered. All the blood in her veins stirred and pulsed at his touch. She turned to face him, leaning back against the counter. She was both tantalized and alarmed by the fire glinting in his eyes.

"You scare me," she admitted.

"There's nothing to be scared of," he answered, his voice husky with desire. "Kiss me, Amanda—don't look away. Kiss me."

She lifted her face to his without protest. She took his mouth hungrily, and his lips enveloped hers in tender warmth. Her arms rose to encircle his neck as he moved his lips against hers, tasting their sweetness. She felt the strong length of his muscular body move closer, felt his warm hands trace slow circles at the small of her back. The tip of his tongue traced the outline of her lips, exploring every inch of their curved softness before parting them gently.

A jolt of voluptuous sensation sped through her as his tongue found hers. She pressed her breasts against his chest, her hands gripping his neck more fiercely, her fingers moving through the silken thickness of his hair. Her mouth clung to his, opening wider to the explorations of his questing, hardened tongue. With a low, passionate moan, she ran her hands down his broad back, delighting in the feel of the muscles rippling beneath her fingertips.

His lips broke from hers. She saw him gazing at her tenderly through a dim mist of desire. "Are you still scared?" he whispered.

She shook her head. There were so many things about him to be wary of—his fame, wealth, and power, the vaguely threatening unknown of his former marriage with its untimely end—but it was her own feelings that frightened her the most. Looking at him, she felt there was nothing casual about their relationship by now. There couldn't be; the feelings were too strong.

She looked away. Ethan gently brushed his lips across her lowered eyelids. She wondered if he, too, was feeling more than merely a physical desire...

"I want to get to know you," he said quietly, as if answering her unvoiced question. "I told you last night that I wanted to take time... and I mean that. In every way."

His lips darted softly down her cheek to rub across her parted lips. Time. Just before she closed her eyes, lifting her face to lose herself again between his lips, the clock on the wall behind him swam into focus. She pulled away.

"Ethan, in less than twenty minutes, forty-two poetry students are going to be wondering where their teacher is."

He looked shocked. In a way, she was almost pleased to be turning the tables after what had happened Friday night.

"I don't suppose you could call in sick?"

She shook her head. Ethan sighed. Then he slowly let go of her and leaned back against the kitchen table. He brushed his hair back from his forehead and glanced at the clock. "Less than twenty minutes?"

"Uh-huh." Amanda gathered her robe about her. "I'm going to take a quick shower and get dressed. Do you think you could give me a lift across campus?"

He nodded. "Think I'll wait for you outside."

"Afraid to try my coffee?"

He smiled, lifted the cup, and took a swallow. He savored it, then set the cup down. "No, it's delicious. What I'm afraid of is staying in this room, knowing you'd be walking around naked with just a wall or two between us. I'm liable to try and jump into that shower with you . . . and then you'd never make your class."

The image sent a little chill of excitement down her spine. "You're right," she told him. "Go away."

He chuckled, and she walked quickly from the kitchen, feeling unsteady on her feet. She showered and dressed in a vague erotic haze.

Only when she was nearly a block from the West Building, sitting next to Ethan in his Thunderbird, did she realize she was starving. "You've made me miss my breakfast," she told him.

"I'll make it up to you. How about dinner tonight?"

He was pulling up to the small strip of leaf-covered lawn that bordered the ivy-lined edifice. Glancing at her watch, Amanda saw that she hadn't a minute to spare.

"All right. Where?"

"The Buffalo Roadhouse."

She'd never heard of it. "Where's that?"

"Manhattan."

Amanda had her hand on the door handle, ready to climb out. She froze now, staring at Ethan in confusion. "You're joking?"

"I'm serious. In fact, I already booked you a flight."

Amanda opened her mouth, then shut it, too stunned by his audacity to even speak. Then, remembering with a start that she had a class to teach, she got out of the car, shut the door, and leaned in the open window to face him again.

"Seriously crazy is what you are, Ethan. What on earth makes you think I could—or would—want to fly back to New York with you on a moment's notice?"

"Two parts blind desire, one part wishful thinking, and a dash of sheer gall," he said with an amiable shrug. "What would you say if I threw in a hotel room with a continental breakfast, besides?"

"I'd say your little mixture has gone to your head," she told him. She turned from the window and walked quickly toward the entrance of the building. Of all the infernal nerve! she fumed inwardly, nearly knocking into someone as she stormed up the front steps.

It was Deborah Varrone and another student. The two girls were staring at her in undisguised awe. Amanda realized with a sinking sensation that they'd undoubtedly witnessed her arrival with Ethan Taylor. Although no one had known of her meetings with the famous playwright before, she had a feeling the Deermount student body was about to receive its first bulletin.

Worse was the lingering feeling of uneasiness that stayed with her as she began to teach her class. Deborah's brooding, myopic stare had reminded Amanda of their conversation about Sono Araki. It was disquieting to think that she still knew so little about the past of this man who was so brazenly pursuing her. A past with the hint of scandal . . .

Toward the end of the class, she looked up from her podium and discovered that she'd gained an extra pupil. Ethan was sitting in the back of the small auditorium. He had slipped in the door at the rear so quietly as to escape notice.

Amanda managed to ignore him for the remaining few minutes of the class. Fortunately for both of them, the students were intent on her words, and at the lecture's end, streamed to the front door for their hasty exit. Only a few glanced curiously at her glowering face as they passed her and followed her gaze to the man slowly walking up the aisle. As they stopped, eyes widening in excited recognition, Amanda shooed them from the room and closed the door behind them with a bang.

"What are you doing here?" She turned on him like a Fury, and he halted midway to the front of the class, holding his hands up in mock-defense.

"I was just curious to catch a minute of you in action. You're fast becoming my favorite institution of learning."

"Very funny. Can I show you the way out now? I've got another class in this room in five minutes."

"Thought about my invitation?"

"At the moment, I'm thinking about manslaughter."

Ethan shook his head in dismay. "Why is it that every time I ask you to go somewhere with me, you act like you've been insulted instead of invited?"

"Because you don't ask me before you ask me!" she exploded, and he laughed.

"For such a literate lady, you're not making much sense."

"I mean—You know exactly what I mean, Ethan Taylor! Last Friday, you assumed I'd go to dinner with you before you even asked me. Then, after I did go, and you left me high and dry, you were presumptuous enough to assume I'd want to see you the minute you decided to come back! Just because you were crazy enough to fly here in the middle of the night. You theater people are so frivolous. You think you can have anything you want. You think . . ." She was bearing down the aisle, and he backed away. "Now you think—you assume— that I'll just up and fly off with you—what about my classes? What about my own work?"

"Amanda." The honeyed huskiness of his softened tone halted her tirade in mid-march. "I want you," he said. "It's that simple. I'm sorry if you've found me . . . presumptuous. But it's just my way when I want something as badly as I want you." He paused. She was silent, feeling her heart thump loudly in her chest. "Hell, I wish you could know how aggravated I was, having to leave Silver Falls . . . But that's why I want you to come with me. Surely even teachers can take a vacation once in a while. If you were with me in New York, we could finally spend some real time together."

It had been hard for her to believe in the depth of Ethan's feelings for her. She was starting to believe now. But his last words struck an oddly familiar chord, one that echoed dissonantly in her memory.

"Even if I could take the time, Ethan, I think you're forgetting that I nearly married an actor once. Don't you have a play opening in a little more than a week? I think I have an inkling of what that means . . ."

"I do," he admitted. "But that doesn't mean we—"

"It means rehearsals, doesn't it? Long ones with late hours that can take up all of a man's concentration. I've been through it from the other side, the side of those who watch and wait. If pre-opening week was bad for a college production, I can't imagine the hell it must be on Broadway."

"An actor is one thing," he said quietly. "It's not quite that way for the writer."

"Can you honestly say you'd have any energy left to wine and dine me in the midst of all that?"

"Professor, I get energized each time I lay eyes on you."

Amanda sighed. Ethan took a step forward, and now it was she who backed away. "Keep your distance," she warned him. "My reputation on this campus has deteriorated enough as it is."

The door to the classroom opened even as she spoke. Two of her students walked in and hurried to take front-row seats, affecting to be absorbed in taking out pads and pens. Other students could be seen, noses pressed to the door's window, staring in at them.

"Much as I'd love to put you in a compromising position," Ethan said softly, "now's not the time or place. So—" as a few more students entered, he gently turned Amanda around and faced her with his back to them. "Meeting me at the airport?"

"No way."

"Okay." He smiled. "I'll call you before I go."

The telephone was ringing as she walked into her apartment at the day's end. She had less than an hour to get ready for Sherman McGuinness's poetry reading, and she considered disconnecting the phone. But then, warily, she answered it.

"This airport sure is lonely just before sundown." The measured, musical crawl of Ethan's voice quickened her pulse. A tension that had been building in her all afternoon broke. She realized that despite all her misgivings, she'd been anticipating his call with longing.

"Wait a second, I'll get out my violin," she said.

"I take it you've had no change of heart?"

"I'm afraid you'll have to cancel my reservation."

"I wish you'd cancel your reservations about coming with me," he said.

His persistence was getting to her. Walking back from campus, she'd even begun evaluating the amount of work she had to get done that week. About how it was out of the question to even think in terms of finding someone to take over her lecture course for the next two days. A part of her wanted to not think at all, to let him just whisk her away, consequences be damned. The effort of trying to sort it all out with his seductive voice at her ear was beginning to bring a dull throb to her temples.

"I don't mean to pressure you." Once again, he was nearly telepathic where her feelings were concerned. "Listen, the play opens next Sunday. Why don't you come for the weekend? Surely you have those off. Look, why don't we take it a day at a time? I'll call you tomorrow. See how you feel."

She could hear the hollow, metallic sound of the airport's PA system in the background. He was leaving again. Would he really keep calling? She had a mad impulse to tell him to wait, she'd join him there, they'd take the next flight. What did she have to lose?

Everything. "You'll call tomorrow?"

"I'll call until you come to me, Amanda. Or until you

tell me that you know you never will."

She exhaled slowly. "I'll sleep on it," she said.

"Have sweet dreams," he said, and was gone.

Sherman McGuinness's reading was a qualified success. The lecture hall was two-thirds full, but those present responded with respectful enthusiasm to the poet's crisply cadenced sampling of his work. Amanda started out attentive. But after a few poems, she began to find the style she'd so admired in the past too dry, too pat, and too solemn. Soon she was pursuing poetic thoughts of her own. Her imagination, inspired by random phrases, spun off on fantastic tangents that were often vividly erotic—and all involving Ethan.

She was glad the poet didn't ask her more than generally how she'd enjoyed the evening when he approached her afterward, at the reception in Hutchins's study. She managed to disengage herself from McGuinness smoothly enough by introducing him to Dean Chast. The two men turned out to be a perfect match.

"I've heard of dueling banjos," Claudia said to her, sipping her white wine as the two women stood in a corner close by, observing the dean's gesticulations. "But this is the first time I've seen dueling windbags."

Amanda laughed, but then quickly sobered her expression at the dean's approach. "I like that man's mind," he announced to her, sotto voce, watching the poet sign an autograph. "I've decided to speak to him about the residency. I'm glad we came up with him as a possibility. That Taylor fellow appears too busy to give us a firm decision. I haven't heard a word from him, and I told him we had a deadline . . ." He furrowed his brow at her significantly, then immediately turned, smiling to greet a fellow administrator.

"What's he mean, 'we'?" asked Claudia, who knew of Amanda's meeting with Chast and Hutchins.

"It would be just like him to take full credit for my idea if the residency goes to McGuinness." Amanda sighed. So Ethan hadn't responded at all? She supposed he *had* been busy, then . . .

"Well, at least then you'd be getting what you wanted," said Claudia, fixing her cool gray eyes on Amanda. "Wouldn't you?"

The difficulty of giving Claudia, or herself, a truthful answer to that question kept Amanda staring at the ceiling above her bed a good portion of the night. The following morning she decided that Claudia would be a much more lively and insightful sounding board than her ceiling, and she called the painter at her on-campus studio.

"If you don't mind talking while I prime the largest canvas I've ever been crazy enough to attempt," she said, "come on by."

Claudia's studio was the top of a reconverted barn whose lower rooms made up the Deermount Art Department. One side of the eaved roof was solid glass. Amanda squinted at the glowing whiteness of the loftlike room's vast interior as she reached the top of the stairs. Claudia was seated on the floor in a pair of overalls spattered with every hue in the rainbow, her hair pulled back, staring at a blank canvas that nearly covered the wall opposite her.

"I think I'm letting myself in for a lot of trouble," she told Amanda. "A commitment to something as big as this means I'm quadrupling my chances of screwing up."

Amanda smiled. "That sounds exactly the way I feel about Ethan Taylor."

Claudia nodded. "All right, Amanda. I've got to cover this thing with gesso—you know, the white base. It's pretty mindless work. So go ahead, just start from the beginning. And don't leave out a single detail."

When Amanda had brought her friend up to date a half-hour later, the canvas was covered with primer. Setting her brush aside, Claudia heated up some mint tea for them on her little hot plate. Then the two women sat, tea in hand, on the brightly hand-painted pillows at the loft's far end where the skylight's glare was softer.

"Let's be pragmatic about this," Claudia said. "You don't have a class Friday afternoon, right?" Amanda shook her head. "Well, that means you could sleep with a celebrity and criticize the latest in contemporary theater in one long weekend—all expenses paid, I take it? Not bad."

"You call that being pragmatic?" Amanda cried. "I barely know the man. I've never been to New York City. And—and I don't own a single thing I could wear to a Broadway opening!"

Claudia laughed. "Now *that's* a practical point, though easily surmountable. As for the rest—"

"Besides, accepting an invitation like this . . . It feels so blatant, like I'm saying, Pull down the covers, here I come!"

"Honey, what's been going on with you and Ethan Taylor hasn't exactly been subtle, if your description does it justice. You're two consenting adults, and you know where it's been leading. What's wrong with that?"

Amanda silently pursed her lips. "It's the afterward, isn't it?" Claudia asked gently. "I'd say you sound like you're half-head-over-heels already. I can see how the final plunge could make you nervous."

"It's *who* he is, too," Amanda said, nodding. "Even the thought of stepping into that theater world of his gives me the shakes."

"Look," said Claudia, setting her glass down with a sharp clunk of conviction. "What's giving you the shakes, when it comes to theater, is a ghost by the name of Brad Sonders. From what I can tell, the only thing he and Ethan have in common is their professions. Taylor's no slave to success—he's got it, and he seems to barely acknowledge it. He's older, too—"

"—and wiser, I'm sure. I know, Claudia. I've gone over the same comparisons." Amanda sipped her tea, thinking. "But then there's his past..."

"Ah, yes," said Claudia, her brow furrowing. "I know a bit about Sono Araki. Well," she said in answer to Amanda's look of surprise, "she was taken quite seriously, even in the art world. Araki was one of the first set designers to bring contemporary modern painters into the legit theater. She once commissioned Warhol to do a backdrop for her, and her own later works got written up in all of the classic books on theater art. I gather she was influential in getting Taylor started in New York."

"And?" said Amanda as Claudia hesitated.

"And, yes, I remember that when she died, there was an ugly rumor floating about that Ethan Taylor had something to do with it."

"You mean he drove her to it?" Amanda exclaimed.

"Well, when a prominent artiste takes her own life without giving her inner circle—or the press—a clue as to why she did it, any mud that's slung is apt to be directed at the nearest logical target, like her husband. Especially if that husband is a current cause célèbre with an annoyingly untarnished reputation."

Amanda let out a deep breath. "I see."

"Actually, from what I understand, the two of them were very close," Claudia said. "Apparently he was really shaken when she died ... as was the theater world," she added. "Araki was a prominent personality—and a tough cookie, I hear." She smiled sympathetically. "I'm not trying to upset you. I'm telling you all I know so that if you do get in any deeper, you won't be hit with hearsay unprepared." She drank the last of her tea. "But that was two years ago," she said brightly. "And from what you tell me, the widower is no longer bereaved. In fact, he's up for grabs—yours, to be precise." She rose. Amanda followed her over to her workspace. Claudia examined the thick layer of paint drying on her canvas.

"If Ethan does get the residency, I could wait and get to know him better in the summer," Amanda mused. "I'm sure he could have it if he could get it together to accept. . . . Actually I was thinking of going over to Max-anne's this weekend for a haircut. It's gotten way too long—" She stopped, meeting Claudia's withering stare.

"You know," Claudia said with an exasperated sigh, "rumor has it there are some decent haircutters in New York City. And clothing stores, restaurants—you know, civilization? It would do you a world of good to get the hell out of Silver Falls for once." She gave Amanda a critical once-over. "Meeting Ethan Taylor's already put a long-lost bloom in your cheeks. And if you think I'm going to sit around this weekend, watching you make long faces because you know you made a big mistake, forget it!"

He called early that afternoon. "There's a TWA flight leaving Dayton Friday at six-oh-five," he said cheerily without even a hello, "and then another at seven-thirty. Maybe you'd prefer the non-stop United flight that gets in at Kennedy at nine o'clock sharp—"

"Ethan," she interrupted, "you're doing that assuming thing again. I still haven't made up my mind."

"Sorry. I thought if you knew how convenient it was, the decision might come easier."

She could picture him smiling as he said it, all six feet of him. She had a sudden searing ache to be in his arms.

"Not tonight," she told him, nonetheless. "But I'm beginning to think about the weekend. *Maybe*," she said quickly. "Just maybe. I don't want to give you the wrong impression."

"It's Wednesday, and you've gone from a 'no' to a 'maybe,'" he observed shrewdly. "That's a right enough impression for me."

Early Thursday morning he called again, once more deluging her with the times of outgoing flights and this time listing salient details.

"The American flight at six has a particularly good menu," he told her. "You've got your choice of salmon steak or chicken—"

"You really do have a pretty lax schedule, don't you?"

"No," he chuckled. "Just a very amenable and efficient production staff. You want to know the name of the first-class steward on United flight 505?"

Still she gave him a maybe. But inwardly the battle was nearly won. When he hung up, she sat holding the phone humming in her lap. She was feeling an emptiness that had a delicious tang of expectation in it. It had been a long time since she'd missed someone other than Brad, and this kind of lonesomeness was a clean one, untainted with bitterness. Amanda realized that as she sat there, she was eyeing her wardrobe through the open closet door. What would one wear, she mused, that is, if one were foolhardy enough...

Friday morning she was awakened not by the ringing of the phone, but by a pounding on her door. The telegram said:

> I HAVE TODAY AND TOMORROW OFF. WHY NOT JOIN ME AT MY HOME IN UPSTATE NY. ROOM WITH VIEW, WORKING FIREPLACE, HORSEBACK RIDING AVAILABLE THOUGH OPTIONAL. CALL FOR RESERVATION: 203-547-3182.

Claudia drove her to the airport.

Chapter
6

SHE DIDN'T KNOW if Ethan's overefficient production staff had been responsibile, or if Ethan had thought she'd enjoy the luxury, but Amanda flew to Albany first class. Drinking champagne at four in the afternoon struck her as indulgent, but she'd only had one plastic cupful. It was "complimentary," and after all, she was in an atmosphere of indulgence.

But a vague feeling of discomfort undercut the pleasure of the wide, plushy seat, the "gourmet snack," and the gracious service. She felt she she didn't belong there, up front with the well-to-do. She felt a bit like an imposter. Thoughts of facing the fashionable New York City nightlife kept her from being able to concentrate on the little folder of school work she'd brought along as a sop to her guilty conscience for leaving campus so abruptly. Her sudden flight from the safe security of Silver Falls was like being shot out of a cannon. Her spirits were high, but she was getting concerned about touching ground. Ethan Taylor wasn't exactly a safety net.

The actual landing was smooth. She walked down the disembarkation corridor, bag in hand. Up ahead, a crowd of people waved at their friends and relatives on either side of her.

Amanda looked for Ethan, her pulse accelerating. As

she realized he wasn't among the throng in the waiting area, her apprehension increased. Maybe he'd had second thoughts, or gotten waylaid, or—

Then he was there, striding towards her in tight, low-slung jeans, flannel shirt, and the familiar corduroy jacket. She had an impulse to run to him that she had to force herself to check. She slowed her pace, feeling her heart thump with increasing force the closer he came. Now she could see the glint of warm welcome in his eyes, the start of a lazy grin easing its way across his lips. He reached out, his hand closing over hers, warm and vibrant, as he took her bag from her. A dizzying jolt of excitement coursed through her. They stared at each other for an infinity of seconds. Then he gently cupped her chin with his other hand and kissed her. It was short, and sweet, but it sent enough blood rushing to her head to make fainting seem not an outlandish possibility.

"What did you pack, Professor? A complete set of Proust?" He grunted in mock dismay at the weight of her canvas bag.

"An iron," she admitted, adding as she sensed his grin broadening: "Don't ask me why, I just did. I'm not used to this spur-of-the-moment traveling. I've probably got everything I don't need in there, and not a thing I do."

"Well, you're here, Amanda, and that's what counts." He put her bag down, and his hands came up to gently grip her shoulders as if he were assuring himself that she was really there. She felt a lump grow in her throat as she read in his face his joy at seeing her again. Then he let go of her abruptly, glanced around him, and cleared his throat. "Did you bring any other bags?"

Her shoulders shook from his touch. She was disappointed that he hadn't taken her into his arms for a longer kiss, but sensed he wanted to be out of this public place. He could kiss her longer later, she realized. She felt a tremor of erotic anticipation at the thought. "No, I traveled light—relatively light," she amended as Ethan picked up her bag again.

They walked through the lobby to its glass doors, then into sunlight and crisp, cold air. Amanda could see her breath before her. Silently in step with Ethan, she felt that subtle electric buzz she was almost—but not quite— getting used to feeling in his proximity. Shading her eyes against the sun's glare, she recognized the glimmering contours of Ethan's Thunderbird.

"Don't tell me you have two of them."

"One in every state," he said straight-faced. Then, seeing her startled look, he laughed. "Kristin drove it back to Manhattan after I flew in. She's got an apartment on the West Side. I picked it up from her"—he was opening the door for her—"and here we go."

Soon the car was gliding down a blacktopped highway lined with pine forest. Amanda glimpsed distant mountaintops through gaps in the trees. So far New York looked much like Ohio, only hillier.

"New York City is a tiny island of concrete that floats off the coast of a great big chunk of countryside," Ethan said as if monitoring her thoughts. "Where I live, there's not a skyscraper in sight, thank goodness. I think you'll like it." Somehow Ethan had known that spending time with him at his woodsy retreat would be easier for her than being hit with the culture shock of Manhattan, and Amanda was grateful for his sensitivity.

"Do you really have horses, or was that just an enticing promotional gimmick?"

"You should know I don't go in for false advertising,"

he said. "I've got two. Do you ride?"

"I've done it once or twice." And loved it, she might have added. She'd always wanted to ride a horse through acres of woods with a tall, dark, handsome stranger. The thought of having one of her childhood fantasies fulfilled quickened her heartbeat. "How is it going with the play?" she asked him.

Ethan rubbed his chin. "At the moment, I've lost my perspective. Casey says the rewrites are working. The producers are happier . . ." He shrugged. "Some reporters snuck into yesterday's rehearsal."

"You must've loved that."

He smiled. "They were trying to pass themselves off as stagehands. One got tripped up in some cable and almost brought down a bank of lights on Anna—she's the lead. I nearly tossed the guy out myself."

"That would have looked good in the papers," she commented, and Ethan chuckled. "So you've got a woman in the leading role. That's a change of pace for you, isn't it?"

Ethan glanced at her. "It is, as a matter of fact. Could it be possible that Miss 'Theater is Dead' Farr has actually read a play or two of mine recently?"

"I skimmed a few," she said.

"What did you think?"

"You're not bad," she said. "Your grammar would give Funk and Wagnall heart attacks, but I kind of like the way you write."

Ethan laughed. "I'm going to take that as high praise. I kind of like the way you think, Amanda." He looked at her. "And the way you look . . ." he added. She'd worn a skirt of chestnut brown and a matching jacket over a cream-colored silk shirt. His eyes lingered on her long enough to start up that voluptuous flush of warm arousal within her again. Then he looked back to the road, asking casually, "Did you pack some sweaters? It gets pretty cold in my neck of the woods."

"I brought one." She had also packed, at the last minute, a pink satin camisole with embroidered lace and matching tap pants—the one extravagant set of lingerie she owned, and rarely used. But that was for later. Amanda shifted in her seat. Later . . . She was feeling comfortable with Ethan; in an odd way, it was as if they already knew each other well. But thoughts of the night ahead did nothing to diminish her inner skittishness.

The countryside outside her window had gotten hillier with fewer signs of civilization. Ethan turned the car off the main highway and up a steeply inclining dirt road. The area was thick with underbrush and tall pines, their trunks glowing purple in the setting sun. The unmarked road lurched over a rise. She heard gravel fly beneath the T-bird's wheels. Then she glimpsed tall brown mountain peaks ahead, beyond a valley of autumnal rust.

"Where are we?"

"East of Woodstock in the Saugerties. My land's near the Massachusetts border."

The took a sharp turn. The car slowed, then rose again on a winding one-lane road. A flock of birds wheeled and banked in formation above the clouds of dust kicked up by the tires. The scenery was even more densely wooded as they ascended, until at last the land leveled and she saw Ethan's house in a small clearing before them.

It was an oversized cottage, two stories high, with a stone chimney and attic gables that glinted white in the sun's glow. Something about the building's solid, simple majesty—the thatched roof, arched windows, huge oaken door—reminded her of a century gone by.

Ethan parked at the end of the gravel driveway. Amanda got out, and as she walked across a carpet of dry pine needles, inhaling the scent of pine mingling with that of burning wood, she was already falling in love with the place. It reminded her of a mill from Thomas Hardy, transported across the Atlantic. Stately pines hovered protectively over the home, which appeared so rooted in the ground it seemed to have grown right out of it. A vast spidery network of vines covered the walls like a natural shawl.

"Ethan, what a lovely house—it's like something out of a storybook!"

"Yes, it is a sort of Yankee Brothers Grimm, isn't it?" he said, leading her up the path of round flagstones. "There used to be a mill on the property. The place dates back to the mid-eighteen-hundreds."

He opened the arched front door for her. Within was a magnificent, huge fireplace of natural stone. The living room was sparsely furnished. There was a low-slung leather couch and an easy chair on a thick burgundy rug in the middle of the hardwood floor. The walls were knotty pine, and the ceilings had large exposed wood beams. Her eye traveled the room's length to the far wall, which was solid glass.

She walked toward it, drawn by the vista of forested mountainsides. Ethan joined her at the window. The house was on a sloping bluff, and the entire valley below lay faintly glimmering in the last of the sun's rays, the majestic mountains that ringed it turning shades of navy blue-green and purple.

Amanda realized that her mouth was open. "My God."

she said. "You get to look at this all year round?"

"It's something I've never taken for granted," he said quietly. "But I feel doubly lucky, getting to see it again as if for the first time—with you."

She turned, feeling his gaze upon her. The dying sun backlit his head with a fiery red halo. She felt the soulful glow of his eyes pull her toward him as he stepped closer. Then slowly, carefully, he brought his lips to hers in a kiss she'd felt coming before it began, a kiss she'd yearned to feel for hours, days.

His arms slipped around her, pulling her into the pulsing warmth of his chest. Amanda drank in thirstily the sweetness of his tongue encircling hers. The rush of desire she felt mushrooming in her body was overpowering. Their lips parted and met again, and a shudder ran through her from head to foot.

Ethan lifted his lips from hers. He looked questioningly into her eyes, his hand softly stroking her cheek. "Let's take it slow," he said. "Now that we've got the time to take our time."

She nodded, her lips still parted in breathless arousal. "I want to make you feel as beautiful as you look to me," he murmured, lightly kissing a half-circle around her upturned face. "But at this moment, it's against my better judgment..."

Now it was she who pulled him closer, her arms hugging him tightly to her. She felt her heart beating against his chest as he stroked her hair. Resting her head on his shoulder, she watched the sun begin to slide below a mountain's craggy peak. The sky was rippled with streaks of red and gray clouds.

"Did you eat on the plane?"

"Couldn't," she admitted.

"Think you could now?"

"Maybe."

Keeping his arm around her, Ethan walked her slowly across the floor. They paused at the bottom of a winding, wooden staircase opposite the front door.

"Go straight down the hall from the top of the stairs, and you'll find the place to put your things. I'm going to see what I can put together in the kitchen for us."

"You cook?"

"Badly," he said. "But there's some good wine in the house that should make up for my ineptness."

A soft, thick gray carpet covered the second floor, as well as the bedroom at the hall's end. Amanda stood in the doorway, admiring the big brass bed that had a colorful down quilt over it. Then she closed the door behind her. Ethan's bedroom was as sparsely furnished as the downstairs, with one painting of rolling farmlands hanging opposite the bed that she recognized, with a start, as an original Grant Wood. The small night table by the bed held an antique copper lantern, a bowl of grapes, and a worn copy of some verse by Yeats. Amanda smiled at the familiar book, a staple of her own library, then set her bag on the bed.

The bathroom that adjoined the room had an old-fashioned porcelain tub in it and a more modern shower attachment. Amanda decided to take a quick shower and freshen up. She found an outlet, plugged in her iron, pulled some clothes from her bag, and stepped into the bathroom.

Through a little beveled window by the tub, she could see the dusk falling over the pines. The soap smelled of wildflowers. As she washed her hair, she felt somehow like a virginal bride preparing herself for a nuptial night.

The dress she'd selected for the evening was sheer. Its wide neckline scooped left to reveal one shoulder. Feeling a bit daring, she put on silk underwear and did without a bra. As she descended the stairs, the rose-colored material clung to her figure, and her nipples were outlined, stiffening in the cooler air.

She entered the kitchen, admiring the rustic detailing of the spacious room, the copper kettles hung above counters of handcarved wood. Ethan was bent over the broiler of an old gas stove. Amanda watched with amusement as he dashed some salt and papper over two steaks and hurriedly shut the door after them. The man was obviously no chef.

He turned and, seeing her, raised his eyebrows at her attire. "Let's drink to the single sexiest shoulder I've ever seen," he said. He handed her a glass of wine and picked up the other he'd poured. She smiled at the compliment and sipped the chablis, savoring its taste.

"You eat out a lot, Ethan?"

"What makes you say that?" He lifted the lid of a pot steaming on the stove and poked at its contents with a fork. "New potatoes," he announced. "My own recipe. You boil them in water and serve them with butter."

"What a novel idea," she laughed.

As it turned out, the steaks were cooked and seasoned decently. They ate together at a long redwood table in the adjoining dining room by the glow of two glass-paneled candle lanterns. The only problem with the meal, she discovered, was eating at all. She was too distracted by the throbbing in her blood, the mounting excitement she was feeling as the evening's inevitable intimacy with Ethan approached.

"Steak too tough?" he inquired innocently. Amanda

realized she'd been chewing the same piece, unable to swallow it, for over a minute. She swallowed now.

"No, I'm sorry," she told him. "It's delicious, really. I'm just not that hungry."

He looked at her. Amanda had the feeling her insides were being X-rayed by his probing eyes. His warm hand closed over hers. "Though I'm deeply offended by your disinterest in the cuisine," he joked. "I wouldn't be averse to finishing up our meal by the fire, myself."

He'd chopped a fresh cord of wood, and Amanda watched him pile it into the great stone hearth while she sipped her wine.

"Kick your shoes off," he suggested over his shoulder.

Amanda hadn't realized that the furry white rug before the fire was a genuine animal pelt, but now she saw the bear's head facing toward the window and its outstretched paws. "Shoot it yourself?"

"No," he chuckled. "It was a gift from a friend. At first I thought it was the corniest thing I'd ever seen, but I've found it to be a real comfort to cold toes."

Amanda took off her shoes and sat down on the floor behind him, leaning back against the low leather couch and stretching out her legs. The soft white fur did feel wonderful beneath her arched feet. She flexed her toes in the downy fleece. Ethan was lighting the kindling. In moments, the wood was a crackling blaze.

He sat down beside her then, lazily unlacing his own shoes. He removed them and his socks. Amanda realized that watching him perform this rather mundane act was deepening the flush that the wine and the fire had already brought to her cheeks. As his feet stretched out close to hers, the heat building up inside her was nearly too much to bear. She stole a glance at Ethan. He was gazing into the fire, seemingly calm and relaxed. How could he be? She felt that being this close to him was sending ripples of erotic tension from her toes to her hair.

"More wine?"

She looked down at her glass and saw it was nearly empty. She nodded. Ethan reached across her to pick up the bottle at her side. As he did, his bare foot accidentally grazed hers. She flet a tiny electrical shock. He paused, still leaning over her. They exchanged a wordless look. Amanda saw a spark of vibrant desire illuminating the velvet depths of his eyes.

"I think the wine can wait," he said softly. "But I can't."

His hand moved from the wine bottle to gently grasp her shoulder as his face came closer, his lips seeking hers. Just before their mouths met, she saw the fire dancing in his eyes. Then the fire was within her as he gathered her to him in a powerful embrace and with exquisite tenderness, softly parted her moist lips with his.

He gently stroked her lustrous hair as his mouth roamed with unrestrained passion over hers. His tongue was eager. Amanda's blood surged in response. Carried away by the aching sweetness of his ardor, her hands slid through his thick, soft hair and her arms pulled him closer, her breath coming in little gasps of pleasure.

Ethan suddenly leaned back, carrying her with him. Her hair spilled across his shoulder as her breasts pressed against his chest, her legs slid into line with his, their tongues enmeshed in a wet, soul-searching kiss. As a voluptuous warmth blossomed in her loins, she moaned into his mouth and pulled him back with her so that the rolling of their bodies continued. They now lay side by side on the rug, hands feverishly gliding over each other.

To kiss was not enough. She wanted to be fused with his body.

"Amanda," he breathed huskily. "I want you . . . now, All of you."

"All of me is yours," she whispered.

He smiled. He leaned forward then and pressed his lips to the base of her neck, his tongue giving the soft skin a whispery flick. As his hands slid the material down farther past her naked shoulder, he nibbled a slow, searing path across it. She arched her back, a shuddering sigh of desire escaping her lips. He answered with a muffled, passionate groan as his hand at last cupped the quivering mound of her naked breast, and his mouth kissed its way along her throat to reach her ear. As his teeth gently bit her earlobe, his hand closed around her breast, thumb and forefinger squeezing her stiffened, aching nipple. She felt fiery arousal streak deep into the core of her like an inner shooting star.

"Ethan," she breathed, her eyes closing. She felt his weight shift slightly, felt the hard outline of him pulse against the soft hollow of her thighs. He covered her face with soft, wispy kisses. The feathery touch continued down her neck until his lips found its silken hollow. He paused, and she opened her eyes. She saw his eyes shining as he gazed at her with rapt devotion.

"Love," he said softly, "you look gorgeous in this dress, but it's got to go."

He helped her up into a sitting position. As he reached to undo her belt, she went for the buttons of his shirt, and they both smiled at the eagerness of their race to undress each other. Once his shirt was undone, she was unable to resist running her hands over the curly tangle of dark hair on his broad chest. Then Ethan pulled her dress up over her head and off; she was tugging at his belt and zipper, his hands were sliding her silk panties down her legs, all in a flurry of erotic haste. At last they were naked, stretched out on the soft white rug, the fire throwing dancing shadow patterns across their skin.

Ethan's eyes roved wonderingly over her body. "You're my dream come true," he murmured. "I hardly know where to begin . . ." She felt her arousal deepen as he bent to slowly trace a wet, warm path of kisses down between the soft valley of her breasts. And then his lips closed around the tip of one breast, his tongue lightly circled her nipple, and she felt a surge of pure pleasure ripple through her.

"Oh, yes," she sighed. "Yes, Ethan . . ." His strong, warm hands held and gently kneaded both her breasts, and his mouth continued its wet witchery on the aching tip of one and then the other. She arched her back, her head turning from side to side as his mouth descended, moving lovingly over her taut stomach. Her fingers wound into the curls of his hair. His tongue licked a delicate path to the dark tangle of silk at the joining of her thighs, and she felt a moist, hot unfurling there. Then she was filled with a surging pulse of ecstasy, the likes of which no man had given her before in her life.

She pulled his hair, guided him upward, digging her fingers into the smooth skin of his shoulders. His mouth found hers again, and she lost herself in the fierce invasion of his hungry kiss. His hands, moving on her legs and hips, were driving her mad. She raked her nails across his muscular back, writhing against his supple body. She held him tighter, feeling all of him against her, wanting him now inside her. . . . Then he was parting her shivering thighs, his hands guiding her hips to meld with his, and with a tantalizing, exquisitely slow thrust, he was hers.

She gasped. The fire before her upturned face flared suddenly as his body enveloped hers. Their hips locked in a gentle rhythmic movement, and she felt a sweetness, a lifting inside of her that she'd never felt. Ethan was watching her, his eyes glazed with loving desire. His mouth silently formed her name as, shuddering, she pressed the silken core of her to his hardness. She could feel the shifting sinews of his muscles as he moved, her hands circling the small of his back. She felt his warm breath on her neck, felt her own breath shift and synchronize with his as their movement gradually slowed.

He held her, still and silent on the brink of incomprehensible pleasure, looking into the very depths of her with his gleaming eyes as every nerve in her body stretched taut, hovering. She looked back at him, and suddenly in the flickering light it seemed his face was changing. She was seeing him almost as one she had never seen before but had always known. And she recognized the face that adored her as he breathed her name again. It was the face of a lover—her lover, her only lover.

Then, as though he had been waiting for this moment, he seemed to smile with his eyes. The starry fire within them glowed brighter. With an inarticulate moan he gripped her buttocks, bringing her hips surging up to meet his, and suddenly they were one thrashing, passionate being, a flaming tangle of limbs, lips, and tongues. Her fingers curved into a bruising clench on the hardness of his hips, and she arched her back, writhing uncontrollably against the luxurious fur beneath them. Tendrils of electric fire spread through her loins as she called his name again and again. Flames surrounded her, flames in the hair that whipped wildly about her head, fire in the fingers that grasped her trembling shoulders. She was ignited, within and without, spinning as if weightless into a radiant bliss, a sudden, ecstatic pure white burst of euphoria. The fire roared in her ears; then she was tumbling in a shower of sparks into warm, fulfilling darkness...

Slowly her legs slid down past Ethan's hips to rest across the backs of his thighs, and her arms relaxed, dropping away from him, her hands lying limply at the sides of his waist. Slowly she felt the fur returning beneath her back, saw the edges of the room swim into focus, and his face before her. Amanda opened her mouth to speak, but couldn't.

"Hello, Professor," he said, and dipped his face briefly to kiss her nose, her lips and chin. A strand of her hair was caught in the moist corner of her mouth, and he pulled it free. "Are you still with me?"

"Absi-tively," she breathed. "Posi-lutely."

He smiled. "You have a way with words."

She sighed dreamily. "You have a way..." Her fingers tickled the soft hair at the small of his back. He hugged her close to him, and she cuddled her face into his warm shoulder. Then he gently let her down again. She stared at him, slowly outlining his eyebrow with one finger, then continuing down the bridge of his nose.

"What are you thinking?"

She felt his raspy, musical voice reverberate through her as he lay against her. "Well, I'm thinking that I met you once, by the Silver River, and I met you again, in Hutchins's study..."

"Yes?"

"...but I feel like I've just met you again—only

really met you, for the first time. Am I making any sense?"

"Perfect sense." He nodded, then shifted his weight, slowly easing himself off her. He sat up, his bronze body glistening with tiny beads of sweat. "Perfect..." he repeated, his eyes traveling appreciatively over the curves of her body. She felt her skin tingle, and she stretched her arms over her head, content as a cat on the furry rug, unembarrassed, in fact enjoying his admiring examination.

"Now that we've met," he was saying, his fingers lightly gliding along her ribs, lazily encircling one breast. "Perhaps we can get better acquainted."

"Better even?" she breathed. "I mean, even better?"

He smiled, his hand gently stroking her breast, fingers deftly teasing her nipple into hardened arousal. "Umhmm," he said, sliding his hand down her abdomen to the juncture of her thighs.

"Better..." he murmured, "...and the best is yet to come..."

They began again a slow dance of arousal on the rug by the fire. Ethan was alternately gentle with her and exhilaratingly aggressive. This second time, their lovemaking was slower, but the intensity was undiminished, and the pleasure even more rapturous. He kissed, fondled, and caressed her as no man had ever done, bringing her to the brink of ecstasy and back, ravishing her with his beautiful, powerful body, transporting her to new heights of sensual intensity with the tenderest of touches.

At last, spent, they lay entwined in the flickering shadows. Amanda closed her eyes and drifted dreamily in a velvet, smoky haze. When she opened them, she saw Ethan across the room, standing by the wall of glass.

She gazed with a kind of dazed awe at his body silhouetted in the dim moonlight. He was perfectly proportioned with lean hips and broad shoulders, the lines of his muscles long and clean. Then he turned, as if he'd felt her looking at him, and she saw his very human face above the sculptured body smile at her, eyes agleam with mischievous sensuality.

"This is a night of firsts," he said. "Come take a look, Amanda."

"I'm not sure I can walk," she muttered, stretching languidly by the dying embers of the fire. She heard him approach and let herself be lifted to her feet by his strong, agile arms. Leaning against Ethan, delighting in the feel of his warm, naked skin against hers, she went with him to the window. Amanda caught her breath as she looked out.

Fluttering flakes of snow glinted in the moonlight. The entire landscape was alive with the silvery specks, flying in whirling circles in the wind. "First snowfall of winter," Ethan announced. "I ordered it just for us."

They walked arm in arm through the pines, Amanda bundled in a down jacket of Ethan's. The night was beautiful, as was his land, dusted lightly with the silver snow.

"That's Massachusetts across the ridge there," he said, pointing to a line of woods in the clearing below. Amanda nodded, listening with half an ear as he indicated the borders of his property. She was more intent on feeling the special comfort of his arm around her. This was the fulfillment she'd been longing for since she'd met Ethan only a week before. It had felt unnatural to walk at his side without his embrace. Now having him so close beside her felt like the most natural thing in the world. She snuggled into the crook of his arm. She'd never felt so comfortable, not with Brad, not with anyone. She wondered if this happiness would be fleeting, or . . . Ethan was still talking. She tried to catch the end of what he'd been saying.

". . . and that's Outer Mongolia, where I slew a dragon once who was scouring the countryside for beardless writers—Ah! You're back," he grinned at Amanda, seeing her look of startled confusion. "I figured if I was only talking to myself, I might as well keep it interesting."

"Sorry." She kissed his snow-flecked chin.

"Sleepy?"

"A bit."

"How about a nightcap then? Something hot and alcoholic? I've inherited my father's knack for making the perfect hot rum toddy. It's sweet and lethal."

It sounded like a great idea, but back in the warmth of the house, she was suddenly so blissfully worn out that she nearly fell asleep, head propped in her arms on the kitchen counter, as Ethan prepared the Taylor recipe.

She laughingly protested as he swept her into his arms and carried her up the stairs to bed. She didn't protest as he undressed her, however, and she soon found herself aroused into wakefullness again. Their lovemaking, lazy at first but increasingly passionate, postponed sleep for quite some time.

The smell of freshly brewed coffee woke her in the morning. She was alone in the big brass bed. The room was filled with soft white light. There was a tray by the bed with coffee, half a grapefruit, and some buttered toast. She sat up, yawning.

She could see snow-covered branches outside the window. Memories of the night before filtered into her mind. She smiled as she took a sip of coffee, wondering where Ethan might be.

After a bite of toast and fruit, she got out of bed, threw on her robe, and headed downstairs. The house appeared to be empty. She paused by the fireplace, listening to a knocking noise that came from outside. Going to the picture window, she saw that the man of the house was out in the freshly fallen snow, chopping wood in the yard. She watched him for a moment, wondering whether she should knock on the window and wave a hello. Then another, slightly sneaky idea formed in Amanda's mind. Left alone, she could do a little harmless exploring.

She was already familiar with the downstairs so she went back up. She was curious to see Ethan's workroom. She knew he had to have some private place to write, most writers did. So when she came upon two doors facing each other across the hall en route to the master bedroom, she assumed that one of them was undoubtedly the door she sought. She chose the left and turned the knob. A quick glance within conformed her guess.

It was a small study with one window that overlooked the valley and a large, old roll-top desk directly beneath it. There were shelves, but surprisingly they were sparsely populated. She perused the few books there and briefly examined the desk. The cubbyholes were full of pens, erasers, notecards, and other stock of the writer's trade, but the desk itself was neat and bereft of work in progress. The entire room was spartan; no prints or posters adorned the soft gray walls. She was a little disappointed at having gleaned no significant details about Ethan's private habits, other than his fondness for number two pencils.

"No photographing allowed," came Ethan's laconic voice from the doorway behind her. Amanda turned.

"I was just—" she began lamely.

"Looking around? No harm in that," he said with a smile. "Find anything interesting?" He walked over to the desk and gestured at the blank walls. "You'll note a significant lack of tickets sales charts, marketing research graphs—"

"Ethan," she said, "I know you a little better than that by now."

"Yes, you do, don't you?" he murmured. He raised his eyebrows at her suggestively and, grabbing hold of her bathrobe tie, pulled her towards him. Their kiss was soft and deliciously sweet, but she closed her robe against his invading hands.

"Seriously, Ethan, I would've expected a slightly more . . . lived-in working space."

"You mean, messy? Well, I cleaned it up a while ago," he admitted. "The mess got shoved in here." Ethan leaned over and yanked open the closet door. The closet's interior was a mass of stacked manuscripts, cartons, files, and papers from floor to the highest shelf.

"That's more like it," she said. "From first appearances I would've thought your finished work sprang right out of the typewriter, letter-perfect." She leaned into the musty darkness. "Got a scrapbook?"

"Of what?"

"Clippings? Reviews?"

He shrugged. "I did keep some in the early days, but I've thrown them out."

She smiled. "No author could be that ego-less. Didn't you keep any?"

He scratched his head. "Good Lord, it's needle in a

haystack time..." He peered into the closet's depths. "Oh, wait, I know—" Ethan strained to reach over the highest stack and felt around on the top shelf. After a moment he produced a faded, yellowing newspaper clipping that had been glued to some cardboard backing, and held it out to her.

"'Shabby Material From An Inept Taylor,'" she read.

"My first review was my worst," said Ethan. "I hung it up to throw darts at for a few years."

She could see that the entire surface of the paper was covered with little holes and rips, but most of it was legible. She giggled. "Boy, they really went to town on you!"

"Not my best work." He put out his hand.

"No, I want to read this," she told him, moving away.

Ethan chuckled. "Enjoy," he said. "I'm going to build us a fresh fire."

"I'll be down in a minute," she said, engrossed in the critic's scathing witticisms at the young playwright's expense. Ethan gave her shoulder a squeeze and left the room.

When she was done with the review, a work of art in itself, she tried to put it back on the top shelf of the closet, but something blocked its easy placement. Amanda pulled the desk chair over and climbed up. There was one carton on the top shelf. The cardboard review must have originally rested on top of it.

She was about to put the review there when she noticed Japanese characters in faded Magic Marker on the sides of the carton. The little hairs on the back of her neck prickled. Put the review back and get out of this closet, she commanded herself. Instead, she pulled the carton toward her and lifted it. Not heavy. She carried it down with her and placed it on the desk.

Quietly, she lifted the box's dusty flaps. A faint, feminine scent of perfume rose from its contents, which were few. Amanda took a sheaf of glossy photographs from the half-empty box and perused the top photo. She recognized in it the faces of more celebrities of the art and entertainment world than she'd ever seen gathered in one place—a restaurant, she realized—and they were gathered around one person at a banquet table: Sono Araki. Ethan was at the side of the beautiful, expensively attired woman, looking at her with an expression of amused affection as she cut a cake . . .

A wedding cake. Amanda felt a stab of sickening resentment. She flipped the photo over to the next. An opening night, judging by the theatrical poster the two lovers were posed against. They grinned triumphantly. Amanda decided to skip the rest of the photos.

Beneath them in the box was a little bound sketchbook. The rice-paper contents were marvelous, intricate drawings: designs for sets, she supposed. They were fantastic and exotic, beautifully realized with the deftest of pen strokes. And in the back, views of Ethan: profile, frontal, three-quarter portraits. Sono had captured him vividly, but the expressions on his more youthful face were somehow unfamiliar to Amanda. There was a pensiveness, a yearning look in his eyes that Amanda was yet to see. Was it a look of love that only Sono could have drawn from her husband?

She shut the book. In the bottom of the box was a single *Playbill* for *Cry of the Dakota Angels*. The thin booklet opened easily to the middle. There, pressed between the slick white pages, lay a dried flower. It was a freesia, lavender and white. Amanda stared at the lovely,

108 Lee Williams

brittle petals. Gingerly, she shut the *Playbill*.

There was a small packet of letters bound with a red hair ribbon wedged into the carton's corner. But Amanda felt she had played Pandora long enough. With hands that were suddenly trembling, she carefully placed the mementos back into the box. The sound of Ethan's jarringly cheerful whistling came from the hall. She quickly closed the carton's flaps.

"What are you doing with that review, memorizing it?" He stood in the doorway, smiling. But his smile faded as he saw Amanda's stricken look. His eyes traveled to the carton on the desk. Wordlessly, Ethan walked over to her. He examined the carton briefly, then opened the top and peered in at its contents.

Abruptly, Ethan closed the carton. When he looked at Amanda, he seemed as shaken by what he'd seen as she had been. "Where did you find this?" he asked.

She motioned at the closet shelf. He nodded, then lifted the carton, put it back, and shut the closet door. When he faced Amanda again, his features were tense, and his voice stiff. "I'd forgotten that box was up there. Why did you take it down?"

"I was trying to put your review back. I was just moving it out of the way, and—" She was mortified. Why had she looked? But damn it, why did she have to deal with Sono Araki in the first place? "I'm sorry. I didn't mean to..." Her words trailed off lamely.

"What happened to your respect for a writer's privacy?" he said. She felt the barely controlled anger behind his words, and instinctively, she moved away from him.

"Why do you have to be so private?" she lashed out. "We're not strangers anymore! You never talk about—

her. I've told you about my past, but I don't know anything about yours!"

"So you go behind my back? You could have asked."

"I wasn't—I mean—it just happened," she said, frustrated. "The door was open, the box was there—"

"I see," he said coldly. "You mean it's my fault for trusting you alone in here?"

"I said I was sorry!" Her anger boiled up and overflowed. "Look, it won't happen again. You can keep your precious memories to yourself!"

She turned quickly and stalked from the room, down the hall and into the bedroom, flinging the door shut behind her. She stood for a moment, her heart beating furiously. But as the wave of anger subsided, she realized that much as his reactions had infuriated her, she was certainly in the wrong to begin with. She turned back to the door and opened it.

Ethan was standing just outside, his hand raised, about to knock. He looked at her, lowering his hand. As she looked into his troubled eyes, she saw more remorse than anger.

"Let's not fight," he said simply.

"Let's not," she agreed.

He stepped past her into the bedroom and went to the window. She sat on the edge of the bed. He turned from the beveled glass to meet her expectant eyes.

"I'm sorry you came across those things," he said quietly. "I don't blame you for your curiosity, I just wish you hadn't seen them."

Seeing the sadness in his face twisted a tiny knife inside her. "Do you miss her?" she whispered.

He stared at her a moment, his lips set tight. "She's still with me in some ways," he answered finally.

Amanda looked away. "I understand," she said quickly. "The two of you were together a long time. I can't expect your memories of Sono to have evaporated...in the short time we've known each other."

"No," he said frankly. "Some of the memories that have stayed with me aren't easily shaken..."

"What was she like?" She forced herself to ask the question, though she felt that blissful ignorance about Sono might be easier to handle.

Ethan glided a hand through his hair, squinting meditatively. "She was a woman of contrasts," he said at length. "She seemed fragile, delicate—but she was fragile as a wolf," he mused wryly. "Sono was a smart and powerful lady....Above all, she was brilliantly talented—almost too talented. Her work consumed her."

"You worked on many plays together, didn't you?"

"We were well suited."

Amanda felt an inner flinch. Ethan sensed her reaction. "And we had our differences, believe me," he added. He seemed to hesitate on the brink of saying more. He stepped closer to the bed, lifted Amanda's chin with his thumb and forefinger, and looked into her upturned face. The room was filled with sudden sunlight from the window behind him. It was clearing outside. The brightness seemed incongruous with the somber atmosphere in the bedroom.

"Go on," Amanda said.

"What do you want to know?" he asked softly. "Going into details may be difficult—for both of us."

She nodded. The happiness she'd been sharing with Ethan was already seeming precarious, in danger of dissolving. She wished the specter of Sono had never risen between them like this, so soon, and apparently so strong.

What did she want to hear? That Ethan's past life didn't matter? That the woman who had come before her was unimportant? Impossible.

"Is it..." She cleared her throat. "Is it over for you...yet?"

Ethan closed his eyes briefly and shook his head. "That's hard to say," he answered slowly and looked away to the sunlight streaming in the window. Then his eyes met hers again. "When I look at you, I begin to believe it's all behind me," he said softly.

It was so much what she had needed to hear. When he pulled her to him then, her heart ached with a yearning to be safe in his warm embrace. When he kissed her brow, stroking her hair with his gentle hands, all that seemed important was recapturing the intimacy they'd shared. When his lips found hers, she lost herself in the savage sweetness of their kiss. The questions that still lingered in her mind faded as her passion rose, and a fiery hunger for his love overrode her fears...

A winding clay path led to the converted barn that served as Ethan's stable, a few minutes walk from the house. One horse, named Wyatt, was jet black but with a white star on its forehead. The other, Hiro, was ochre-brown. Ethan helped her up onto Hiro's saddle and mounted Wyatt himself.

Soon they were slowly ambling down an open field of white. The horses' ears bristled, their hot breath making clouds in the cold air, their hooves kicking up small sprays of snow. The trees were luminous with tiny icicles as the sun broke through the clouds.

"You'd better drink in this peace and quiet while you can," he told her, reining Wyatt in from a brisk trot to amble slowly beside her. "When we get to New York City, you may wish you could have bottled some and brought it along with you."

Amanda smiled. Ethan seemed his usual cheerful self. As they approached a low-hanging branch, he leaned over to duck her head for her and planted a quick kiss on her cheek. He playfully nuzzled her ear before Hiro snorted and pulled her away.

Cantering beside him through this pristine world of splendiforous nature, Amanda felt the lingering feelings of disquiet she'd had since discovering Sono's belongings begin to lift. It seemed that door was best left temporarily shut. She only regretted not having had a chance to broach the subject of Sono to Ethan in her own time and fashion.

For now, at least, she was willing to let the subject lie. In a few hours, she was going to face Broadway. The unknown that awaited her there was quite enough to worry about.

Chapter
7

THE LINE OF cars behind them honked furiously, but Ethan couldn't move. In front of them, the driver of a white Porsche, a woman wearing mirrored sunglasses and silver earrings the size of baseballs, had tried to run the light on the corner of the city blocks called "Spring Street" and "West Broadway." She had nearly collided with a truck. The truck driver—bearded, ponytailed, in a paint-spattered T-shirt—seemed more interested in inventing new curse words to direct at the Porsche driver than in trying to back up. Ethan sighed, drumming his fingers on the steering wheel of the Thunderbird.

"Maybe Soho on a Saturday afternoon was a bad idea," he said. "But my favorite omelette joint is just down this block."

"Don't worry about me," Amanda told him. "I'm fascinated. Saturday afternoons on the Spring Street in Silver Falls are nothing like this."

The truck-and-sportscar argument had attracted a sizeable crowd of spectators on each corner. To Amanda, it looked as if some movie casting director had ordered one of everything for this New York City street scene. A Japanese businessman in a suit stepped in front of a tall black woman in a paisley dashiki to take a photo of the truck driver. Two teenage boys with matching red-and-blue-streaked spiky hairdos jostled him in passing and nimbly sidestepped a young couple in blue jogging sweats pushing a baby carriage. The mustachioed, balding proprietor of the fish store on the corner, just emerging from his doorway, greeted the couple. Wiping his hands on his apron, he bent down to smile at the baby in the carriage. Amanda noted that this towheaded little cherub wore a jogging outfit that matched his parents'.

At last the truck driver finished his tirade, and the traffic moved. Amanda gazed in rapt curiosity at the passing parade of tall, ornately detailed loft buildings that housed art galleries and fashionable clothing boutiques. The sidewalk show of cosmopolitan color and style seemed circuslike to her.

Ethan spotted a parking place and swerved quickly to nab it. Amanda grabbed the dashboard as he maneuvered the T-bird, expertly wedging into what had seemed like a too-tight spot in one quick move. "Zen and the art of city parking," he grinned as she shook her head, impressed.

Up the street was a low building that looked like a reconverted diner, which in fact it turned out to be. The Sundance Diner was a clean, well-lit place with an old-fashioned black-top counter and silver swivel stools. The clientele was young and casually dressed. Ethan and Amanda slipped into the one vacant table at the back of the long, one-room restaurant. Sun slanted in through the blinds on the windows, and the hanging potted plants in the corner threw leafy patterns of shadow across their quiet niche.

Ethan reached across the table to squeeze Amanda's hand. "Tired?" His eyes probed hers with a soft and glowing concern. The one word conjured up images of the long night they had spent together. She felt her body suffuse with heat as she vividly recalled the reasons for their both getting very little sleep.

She nodded. "I like this kind of tired," she said softly. Her face flushed as he lifted her hand to his lips and kissed it.

"Me, too," he murmured. She could tell from looking in Ethan's eyes that he was sharing her thoughts. He smiled. "That was a particularly breathtaking . . . sunrise, wasn't it?"

"Menus?"

Ethan looked up and greeted the waitress with a friendly nod. Though his hand let go of hers to take the menus from the curly-haired, freckle-faced young woman, his eyes returned to caress Amanda's face as they listened to a recital of the day's specials. They both ordered quickly, having worked up healthy appetites on the two-hour drive from Ethan's home to Manhattan.

The food was good; large portions were placed in artful designs on the plates. Ethan had an omelette with cream cheese and onions, and Amanda tried a more exotic one with salmon. They were enjoying a leisurely cup of coffee at the meal's end when Amanda saw a couple, both blond-haired and ostentatiously dressed, staring at Ethan, then her, from their table nearby. The woman leaned over to her companion. A sibilance in her speech accented one word in their whispered conference. Amanda was sure she had heard Sono's name mentioned. She stiffened apprehensively as the couple rose and approached their quiet corner.

"Ethan! Good to see you, my man!"

Ethan turned, his brow furrowing in obvious displeasure at being recognized. Amanda sensed immediately that these people were not friends of his, but mere acquaintances and not favored ones. The blond woman was openly staring at Amanda, who fidgeted uncomfortably.

"How's it going with the show? You know, I called

Barnaby at the office and couldn't even get a couple of comps out of him! You must have the hottest first night tickets in town." The man's booming voice had now elicited the attention of everyone in the restaurant. Amanda saw Ethan blanch and shoot a longing look at the exit as heads turned and a low buzz of murmured recognition surrounded them.

"David Bock's been asking for you," the man went on.

"How is he?" Ethan asked perfunctorily. "Send my regards."

Thankfully, their waitress materialized with the check, rather brusquely pushing the couple aside to present it to Ethan. "You can pay me now if you like," she informed him, blocking Ethan from the couple's view. Amanda had a feeling the young woman was running interference for him.

"Fine," said Ethan gratefully, taking out his wallet.

The two unwanted intruders withdrew, glowering in annoyance at the impassive waitress. "I guess we'll be seeing you uptown," the man called out. The blond bared her teeth at Amanda in some semblance of a smile, and then the two of them were gone. Ethan paid the waitress, giving her a generous tip.

"Thanks." She smiled, then added, "Good luck tomorrow night."

"Thank you," said Ethan. He ushered Amanda up the aisle. Once in the street he exhaled, shaking his head.

"You really don't seem to like it," she said in wonderment as they walked to the car.

"What?"

"Being famous."

He opened the Thunderbird's door for her. "I can get my plays produced. That's what it's worth to me. The rest is really an embarrassment."

She examined Ethan's rugged profile as he pulled the
car out of the space. "You know David Bock?" she asked
him. Bock was a famous young artist whose exploits as
the bad boy of high society received more attention in
the papers than his paintings.

Ethan nodded. "We used to go to his openings."
Amanda looked away, feeling a tinge of jealousy at his
unconscious reference to his married life. "I never got
to know him well," he went on. "The man drinks too
much."

"Are you a drinker?" She looked at Ethan again. Even
after the intimacy of their weekend together, she was
struck by how little she knew of him. The circles Ethan
had traveled in were foreign, as unreal to her as the photos
of the rich and famous she'd glimpsed occasionally in
magazines.

Ethan smiled as he weaved through traffic. "Almost
never touch the stuff. Well, that's not entirely accurate.
I tended bar in a place on the Lower East Side when I
was first getting started here..."

He began to tell her anecdotes, mostly comic, of his
early days struggling in Off-Off-Broadway. His ability
to poke fun at himself relaxed her somewhat. She felt
he was deliberately attempting to put her at ease. Even
though she knew this, his strategy worked. By the time
they were in midtown, she was snuggled up against him
in the seat, laughing at his stories, content to watch the
unfamiliar landscape of Manhattan glide by.

Chicago had had its share of skyscrapers, but also
many wide open spaces. This city seemed a bewildering
but beautiful jumble of architecture, old and new,
crammed into small blocks that bustled with activity.
Ethan pulled the car into a lot on Forty-Fifth Street be-

tween Broadway and Eighth Avenue. Amanda had to admit that the line of colorful marquees glittering down the block was an impressive sight.

The most impressive to her was the one emblazoned with the name of Ethan's play, *A Fire in the Rain,* in letters a story high on the Summergarden Theater. Ethan paused with her just outside the door that led backstage. He put his hands on her shoulders, looking into her eyes with a gaze of affectionate concern.

"They should post a sign that says, 'Abandon hope all ye who enter here.' " he said. "It's going to be madness in there. Tonight is dress rehearsal, and today is probably—"

"Total hysteria," she finished for him. "You don't have to tell me. I'll stay out of your way."

"I shouldn't be too long. I just have to meet with Casey and see if the line changes have worked. If you get bored, you can check into the hotel ahead of me."

She nodded. He kissed her. Then, within moments, they were in the midst of a melee.

The theater's houselights were up. Innumerable technicians were running in all directions. Conversations were being conducted at rapid-fire speed and screaming pitch all around her. A spotlight roamed the stage as various other colored lights blinked on and off in quick succession. Amanda ducked as two burly men carried a painted flat aloft down the aisle. When she looked up, Ethan was no longer at her side. She couldn't place him for a moment in the confusion of people rushing about the apron of the stage, so she took a seat in the orchestra section. The houselights suddenly blacked out.

Now she saw Ethan at the foot of the stage, having what appeared to be a heated argument with a hawk-nosed man dressed in black who stood on the stage above

him. This man, whose woolly beard and wild mane of
hair seemed to be flying off in a million directions, waved
a clipboard full of papers at Ethan and clutched his heart
as if wounded. Both men at once broke into hearty gales
of laughter. The man in black jumped from the stage,
landing at Ethan's side and clapping an arm around his
shoulder. Amanda surmised that this frizzy-haired, fre-
netic specter was Casey Roberts.

"Scene Four!" Casey yelled. For all of two seconds,
there was a dip in volume in the general hubbub. A man
and a woman appeared from the wings. Ethan leaned
over the edge of the stage and began to confer with them.
Casey turned and strode up the aisle, taking a seat directly
in front of Amanda. Abruptly, he turned to face her.

"Hi. Who are you? How did you get in?"

Startled, she opened her mouth to speak, but he went
on: "You're not with a paper, are you? It's a closed
rehearsal."

"I'm Amanda Farr," she managed to get out. "I came
in with Ethan Taylor."

Casey's eyes narrowed. Then he snapped his fingers.
"The professor from Ohio?" He held his hand out to
shake hers. "Casey Roberts. Did Ethan get any work
done this weekend?" He squinted at her. "Doubtful. Well,
we'll see in a moment. This your first time in the city?"

"Did you drink a gallon of coffee today, or do you
always sound like this?" she asked him, smiling.

Casey's eyes glittered in the darkness. "You're pretty
quick yourself," he grinned. "You here for the opening?"

"Easy on the cross-examination, Casey."

Ethan stood in the aisle shaking his head as Casey
held his hands up in mock surrender. "Sorry, sorry, just
getting acquainted." He whipped around in his seat and
yelled at the stage. "Roma! Jerome! Where are ya?"

Casey rose as some voices floated out of the darkness. "You gave them the new cuts and the monologue?" he asked Ethan. Ethan nodded. Casey zipped down the aisle to hold a conference with the actors.

"Listen," Ethan began, kneeling by Amanda's chair. "It turns out there are a few changes I've got to—"

"I could see this coming, Ethan. It's okay."

He put his arm around her, running his hand through her hair. "It should only take a few hours. I'm sorry . . ."

As always, the touch of his hand on the back of her neck and the caressing gaze of his glimmering eyes combined to stir her blood and quicken her breath—as well as to stifle her budding annoyance. She was being reminded of similar past situations with Brad. But Brad hadn't even been this solicitous with her. And he hadn't had the melting force of Ethan's magnetic charm. "Do you want me to wait?" she said, aware that her voice had grown suddenly husky.

He smiled. "I want you to . . ." he murmured and leaned forward. Just as his lips met hers, the houselights went up again. What might have become a more passionate kiss was cut short. As Ethan straightened up, Amanda saw one of the actresses standing in the aisle behind him.

"Excuse me," she said with a smile. "Ethan, Casey wants you to go over Jerome's monologue with him."

"Okay. You've got the cuts we made in Scene Four?"

"Yes, I think they'll work wonderfully well," she said breathlessly.

Amanda didn't like the way this woman was smiling at Ethan. But even as the thought occured to her, she chided herself for giving in to jealous feelings so easily.

"Amanda, this is Roma."

"Hi." Roma turned her smile on Amanda.

"Hello," Amanda said, feeling a tinge of intimidation. The woman was beautiful, sensuously Mediterranean-looking, with an aquiline nose and big brown eyes accented by exotic makeup. Her hair was a mass of finely coiffed ringlets. Though dressed casually, Roma had an air of cosmopolitan sophistication Amanda had never before encountered firsthand.

"Just a second!" Ethan called to placate Casey, who was waving his arms frantically from the stage. Ethan gave Amanda a rueful grin and sauntered down the aisle. Amanda watched his tall, powerful physique in motion. She enjoyed seeing him in his element.

Roma took a seat behind Amanda. She could feel the woman's eyes on her, sizing her up. Amanda suddenly felt a bit provincial in the simple skirt and sweater she was wearing.

"Gum?"

Amanda turned. Roma was offering her a stick, with a friendly smile. Amanda shook her head but smiled back. She was determined to overcome her anti-actor prejudice. She wanted to like the people Ethan worked with and not prejudge them. "How do you like being in Ethan's show?" she asked Roma.

The actress rolled her eyes heavenward. "The man is a *jean*-yus!" she said. Amanda was amused to hear Roma's broad twang of a New York accent contrast with her exotic veneer. "You couldn't ask for better dialogue. I mean, I'm only in a supporting role, but my part is so well-written that I feel like I've known the character all my life." She looked at Amanda with undisguised curiosity. "How long have you known him?"

"Ethan? Not long really. We met a little over a week ago."

"Wow," said Roma, shaking her head. "And he brought

you upstate? Oh, I'm sorry—" she said, seeing Amanda's startled look. "It's just that no one could believe Ethan was inviting someone to his house—it's his ultra-private domain, and he hasn't had anyone up there since..." She paused uncertainly, then gave Amanda a wide smile. "I don't mean to be nosey. This is your first time in the city, isn't it?"

"Why, is it written all over me?" Her defensiveness was rising.

"No, no," Roma said quickly. "I just had a feeling..."

Ethan had reappeared out of the darkness. "Let's get some coffee," he said to Amanda. "They don't need me for another twenty minutes."

"Nice meeting you," Roma called as Ethan hustled Amanda down the aisle.

"Does everyone here know everything?" she whispered.

"Well, New Yorkers can act sort of snobbish—"

"No, I mean about us."

Ethan chuckled. "People will talk. But why listen?" He put his arm around her. "They'll never know what we know," he said softly and kissed her hair.

Out in the bright sunlight, she squinted at the line of battered taxi, cars, and shiny limousines. Ethan guided her through the throngs of well-dressed tourists attending Sunday matinees. At Broadway, they paused. "There's a place across the street," Ethan mused, then turned to Amanda, his eyes glinting mischievously. "I've got a better idea. How would you like the best iced cappuccino in Manhattan?"

"Sounds great."

"All right then—" He stepped from the curb, put two fingers in his mouth, and let out an ear-shattering whistle.

A cab that had been zooming down the street abruptly swerved across two lines of traffic and screeched to a halt in front of them. It seemed to Amanda he'd missed a three-car collision by a hair's breadth.

They got in the roomy Checker cab. Ethan told the driver to head uptown. The driver nodded and executed a death-defying U-turn that sent Amanda's heart pumping in double-time. She gripped the seat with one hand and Ethan's knee with the other.

"Don't worry," Ethan grinned. "I can tell this is one of the better drivers."

"Better? What are the best? Kamikaze pilots? And where are we going? I thought you only had a few minutes."

"Just in case I get cooped up in that theater for the rest of the afternoon, I want to spend as much time with you as I can now—and I thought you'd want to see more of the city."

"Maybe I should see less and live to tell about it," she muttered, as the cabdriver cut off a car, and horns blared all around them.

"Relax, Professor, and let me be your guide. Up ahead, that's Columbus Circle—" He paused as the cab swerved, pitching Amanda into his arms. "Well, it would've been nicer to sightsee in a horse and carriage . . ." He leaned forward. "Take us through the park—and you can slow down."

From the bustle of midtown, they were suddenly amidst the peaceful, beautiful oasis of rolling lawns and sculpted forestry that was Central Park. Amanda hadn't actually believed that horse-and-carriages were available until they passed a hansom cab, its driver urging on the horse, whose steady clip-clop of hooves echoed on the cobblestones.

"A holdover from a bygone era," Ethan said, seeing Amanda's expression of surprised delight. "This city isn't all just twentieth century. Maybe we'll take one out tonight."

It was a city that seemed to be a dozen cities in one to Amanda. In a moment, they were turning down Fifth Avenue. Its awe-inspiring luxury hotels and the grandeur of Saint Patrick's Cathedral were dwarfed in turn by towering modernistic skyscrapers. Ethan pointed out significant sights. Amanda relaxed in the reassuring hold of his strong arms around her as they zoomed eastward again back uptown a few blocks to a broad, European-style plaza by the East River.

Ethan instructed the cabdriver to wait and helped Amanda out. At an Italian café in the shadow of the futuristic Tramway, he ordered two iced cappuccinos to go. Amanda watched the cable car above them sail slowly across the river to Roosevelt Island in the late afternoon sun. Then the coffees were ready, and they were back in the cab. With a squeal of brakes as they avoided a near-collision with a bus, they headed back across town.

"A nice part of town," Ethan commented as they crossed the solemn luxury of Park Avenue. "Our hotel's not far from here." His voice was soft and seductively caressing by her ear. Ethan slid his arm around her waist as they glided down Fifth Avenue again. "If we had more time, I'd love to check in with you..."

She felt her body strain and tingle in her clothing as he nuzzled her earlobe, his hand softly rubbing her side just below the swell of her breast. "If we had more time, I'd make sure you didn't check out again," she murmured.

"Ever?"

"Well, at least until opening night..." He kissed her

again. She leaned her head against his shoulder. Swank shops of every nationality lined the street that showcased Rockefeller Center's art-deco splendor. Then they were back amidst the tawdry spectacle of Times Square, and suddenly the cab was screeching to a halt in front of Ethan's theater.

Ethan paid the driver and helped Amanda out. "End of the special twenty-two-minute tour," he announced, looking at his watch. "You can sign up for a longer one tomorrow."

"So that's your idea of a quick cup of coffee," she said as he led her to the stage door. "What's the longer tour, a quick bite on a motorbike?"

"Oh, no. No quick bites with you, Amanda. Just long, leisurely meals..." His fingers teasingly stroked a line from the soft nape of her neck to her shoulder as they walked through the darkness, sending a delicious chill down her spine.

Backstage was still a flurry of loud, furious activity. After her high-speed sightseeing, Amanda felt her senses were in danger of being overloaded. "I'll just take a seat and watch for a few minutes," she told Ethan, and he nodded. A number of people, Casey included, were already gesturing at him to join them. Amanda left the playwright's side and returned to her seat in the darkened orchestra section.

She watched Casey take Roma and Jerome through their paces in a scene that had been added at the last minute to replace a cut one. Ethan observed from the foot of the stage, occasionally interrupting to have whispered conferences with Casey over a particular line reading. Was she imagining things, or did Roma seem oddly concentrated on Ethan? Whenever the action of the scene was halted, the actress would watch Ethan and not Casey.

Amanda wondered if her first impression—with its suspicious jealousy—had any foundation. Fleetingly, she thought back to Brad once more. Many times she'd misunderstood a worker's camaraderie between Brad and an actress as being something more, and her jealousy had provoked needless arguments. Let's not go through that again, she told herself. Most probably the young actress was a bit in awe of Ethan and unconsciously playing up to him.

Casey called a temporary break. Ethan turned from the stage and shaded his eyes, looking for Amanda above the glare of the footlights. She rose and went to meet him in the front. He put his arms out and pulled her up onto the stage with him.

"It's your Broadway debut, Amanda," he joked as she gaped at the cavernous darkness beyond the stage. It seemed almost threatening from this vantage point. "It's awesome, isn't it?" he said. "You have to be a secure performer to withstand the pressure of a house this large."

Amanda felt Roma watching them as Ethan walked her to the wings. "I think a certain supporting actress may have a crush on you," she said once they were backstage alone.

Ethan looked momentarily confused. "Roma?" he said. "I hope not. Her boyfriend's an excitable fellow. And besides . . ." He drew her closer to him. "The only crush I care about is this one."

He kissed her, melding her body to his in the twilight of the backstage corner. Amanda responded hungrily to the sweetness of his lips and tongue. She'd never known a man who could excite such a deeply passionate response in her so quickly. His slightest caress ignited an instant flare of desire in her, and she'd given up on trying to hide her excitement from him. Her own obvious arousal seemed to increase Ethan's ardor.

"We can't go on meeting like this," he jested as at last they broke apart.

"Seriously, Ethan, when do you think...?"

He sighed. "Could be a couple of hours."

"I have to admit I'm beginning to feel a little left out and in the way. Maybe this wasn't the best time for—"

He put his finger to her lips, shaking his head, then kissed her softly on the bridge of her nose. "It's been the best time," he murmured. "The best time I've had in a long, long time. I'm glad you're here. I'm only sorry I can't be with you more."

"Are there always so many last-minute changes?"

"No. But a scene that we cut early on has to go back in. The first act hasn't been working without it."

"Maybe I will go back to the hotel."

"Might be less of a bore. I'll miss you, though," he added. "I like knowing you're out there in the darkness."

"I like watching you work with Casey."

"We've been a team for years."

"I was just wondering..." She paused, but then took the plunge. "The way Jerome swears when he leaves the stage at the end of the scene—is that in the script?"

Ethan's eyes narrowed. For a moment Amanda thought she'd crossed another forbidden boundary. But then he laughed, gazing at her with amused affection. "It wasn't in the script originally. It was a piece of business that we've kept in, but I was starting to have doubts about it myself." He held her at arm's length for a moment, his eyes seeming to drink in every detail of her face. "I think I'm falling deeper in love with you by the minute," he said slowly. "I also think you might be a decent editor."

"Taylor! Where the hell are you?"

It was Casey, storming onto the stage behind them. Ethan gave her a quick but fiercely passionate kiss. Then they broke apart. "They need me," he whispered.

She nodded. "And I'll get going."

After she collected her bag from Ethan's trunk, she found a cabdriver who drove slowly but didn't speak much English. He got her to the hotel without any mishaps, though, and Amanda checked in.

The St. Royale was on a relatively quiet block between Madison and Fifth. The lobby had an Old World gentility about it, evincing money and sophistication without ostentation. She admired the carved wood paneling of the elevator as she went up with the elderly operator. He indicated the direction of her room, then smiled politely, shutting the wrought-iron gate behind her. Amanda walked down a high-ceilinged hall, unlocked the door at the far end, and turned on the light switch.

She was in a well-appointed suite of rooms. The sitting room had a marble fireplace and pastel-painted walls with ornate moldings. The bedroom was a corner room with three huge windows. She was high enough to overlook the southeast corner of Central Park, and the dappled brown and gold autumnal vista sparkled charmingly beneath her in the late afternoon light. She pulled the curtains back.

The room was decorated cheerfully in pale blues and greens. The bed was a handsome antique four-poster, the carpet thick and colorfully Oriental in design. In the bathroom, a room the size of her bedroom in Silver Falls, she found a large porcelain tub with oversized European fixtures.

Amanda strolled through the rooms, savoring every detail. There was even a tiny refrigerator in the sitting room's corner stocked with sodas and ice, and a writing desk in the bedroom equipped with fancy stationary and pens. The commodious bathroom looked especially inviting. She decided to indulge herself in a hot bath.

Some twenty minutes later, stretched out in the tub, she felt as pampered as a princess. The hotel had provided some bath powder. She reveled in the light, soapy suds and the flowery scent. The luxury of it all seemed nearly sinful.

The bath soothed and relaxed her so, she felt she could take a nap. But Ethan might be returning within the hour. She opened her bag on the big poster bed and put on the two-piece satin teddy. Ethan hadn't seen her in it yet. Somehow, upstate, their passion for each other had flared so spontaneously, and so often, that she'd never had a chance to change en route to the boudoir. Now she was glad she'd had some time to prepare herself for his imminent arrival.

Stretched out on the soft, comfortable bed, she felt her appearance was in tune with the surroundings. But when she took her folder of school work out of the bag to look at, she was suddenly brought up short. What was Geoffrey Chaucer doing in this romantically elegant suite? For that matter, what was she?

Ethan never flaunted his wealth. She'd assumed he had reserved these lavish surroundings as a gesture toward their being together, and she'd been touched by it. But for a moment she felt guiltily Cinderella-like—an imposter awaiting the toll of midnight. She thought again of that couple in the Soho diner, of David Bock, and the side of Ethan she knew nothing about, the other world where he and Sono Araki had reigned supreme.

Amanda sighed, fingering the folder of papers. She was entitled to her rare weekend of indulgence, and no ghosts of Ethan's past were going to take it away from her. Stifling a yawn, she began to read.

Chapter

8

SHE WAS WALKING down a long, echoing hallway, trying to catch up with Ethan. He was ahead of her, striding quickly toward a shimmering line of distant footlights. Though she walked faster, the distance between her and Ethan was lengthening. She called his name. He kept walking.

A figure stepped in front of her, blocking her path. Amanda recognized the imperious, foreboding woman in black even before she was close enough to make out her delicate Oriental features: Sono Araki.

Frightened, she called out to Ethan again. At last he seemed to hear her and paused in his stride. But the man who turned around to gaze at her expressionlessly, backlit by the stage lights, wasn't Ethan. It was Brad Sonders.

She'd lost Ethan. Where was he? Fear made her pulse pound in her ears. The bell that signaled the rising curtain chimed shrilly—

The telephone was ringing.

Groggily, Amanda pulled herself out of the soft covers of the bed, groping for the phone in the darkness. She hardly knew where she was. Her heart was still pounding as she found the receiver and warily held it to her ear.

"Professor?"

Relief poured through her veins, melting the icy chill her nightmare had given her. "Ethan! Where are you?"

"I'm right where you left me, sweetheart. Are you all right? You sound strange."

She'd found the switch on the lamp by the bed. As the little pool of light blinked on, Amanda read the face of the clock on the night table. Nearly one in the morning. "I was asleep," she said, sitting up.

"I called earlier to tell you I wouldn't be back before dress rehearsal, but you didn't pick up. You must have been out cold."

"I guess I was." She yawned. "Are you done now? These are lovely rooms, but I'm lonely."

"I feel terrible about leaving you stranded there," he said softly. "And I promise you that after tonight, we'll be together for the rest of your stay. Honest. I'm sorry . . . Are you hungry? I'll pick up something."

She did feel hungry, and chilly in her negligee. For a moment she felt crankily incensed at being abandoned.

"Amanda. Are you still talking to me?"

She smiled. "I guess. But I'd rather talk in person. What are my chances?"

"I'm on my way. Do you like Japanese food? There's a place right next to the theater that's got great take-out teriyaki."

She winced, remembering her dream. "Not really. Is there anything else open at this hour?"

"In New York City? What would you like? Italian? Ukrainian? Chinese? Greek?"

"Surprise me. But hurry."

"I'll be there before you have time to get properly annoyed all over again, I promise. Okay?"

"Okay."

When she'd hung up, Amanda rubbed her bare arms, looking sleepily at her surroundings. The ceilings seemed even higher in the dim light. She rose from the bed, put on her robe, then walked to the windows and looked out.

Manhattan's glittering skyline rose from the lamplit darkness of the park. At night, the city looked alluringly lovely. There were cars' tiny headlights still streaming up the streets below, and lights glimmering in the windows of tall buildings on all sides. But the daytime bustle had given way to a slower, softer pace. She could see the moon through a pale wreath of clouds, and the distant blinking lights of airplanes above the skyscraper tops.

She returned her gaze to the shiny streets. Somewhere down there, Ethan Taylor was on his way to her. It felt oddly exciting to be alone, waiting for her lover in a strange hotel in the dead of night.

But as the minutes passed, her excitement shifted to disquiet. Her nightmare came back to her as she restlessly paced the expansive suite. Had she made a mistake in coming, after all? What if he wasn't on his way? He might have succumbed to his work's demands again. She'd been through that before; the phone call after the first phone call, another delay, another apology, then the empty bed, and the morning's argument—

She heard the key in the lock. Without even thinking, Amanda ran to the door, ran into Ethan's arms as he walked in, hugging his body to her with such vehemence that he seemed taken aback as he held her, smiling, by the door.

"That's what I call a warm welcome," he murmured, kissing her ear, running his fingers through her hair.

"I guess I missed you."

"I've missed you, too," he said, his voice soft and husky. Amanda enjoyed the strong, clean scent of him, then stepped back, aware of another smell. Ethan held up the brown paper bag he'd been holding behind her back.

"Paella—shrimp and chicken in Spanish rice. Acceptable?"

"Quite," she smiled.

They walked together to the bedroom. In the light, she saw him more clearly and realized he looked weary. Of course. While she'd slept, he'd been working.

"You must be exhausted."

He shrugged. He looked at her, his eyes roving over the negligee revealed by her open robe. "No," he said slowly, his eyes gleaming brighter in the soft lamplight. He pulled her closer. "Not exhausted at all..."

His kiss was fiercely passionate. Her flesh responded to the fire in him with its own rising flame. Ethan stepped back and pushed the robe from her shoulders. The pink satin seemed to fuel his arousal. With a little groan of desire, he swooped her up into his arms and carried her to the bed.

"Aren't you hungry?" Amanda protested laughingly, her arms tight around his neck.

"Starved," he said. "For you! I want to taste every inch of you, from top to bottom..." She heard a growl in his throat as he kissed his way from her ear to the nape of her neck. He was rough with hunger for her. She revelled in the eager pleasure his hands took as he tore the thin straps of satin from her trembling shoulders. His mouth found her naked breasts and licked and bit them into aching arousal.

Feverishly, she tugged at his clothing, as fired and hasty as he. Once again she gloried in the sight of his broad, beautiful chest, his taut abdomen, and his wonderfully aroused manhood. At last all barriers of clothing were gone. Their hot skin melded in a violent embrace of passion.

A cry of joyous fulfillment escaped her breathless lips as she felt the plunge of him inside her. He, too, issued a small sigh of satisfaction as she wrapped herself around him. They slowed together to savor the sweet, sensual bliss of their union. Their haste gave way to an exquisitely prolonged, teasing exploration of each other's bodies. He kissed her mouth, throat, breasts, shoulders. She bit his earlobe, running her fingers through the curly tangle of hair on his chest, tickling him, then rolling her hips to match his leasurely thrusts.

"Open your eyes," he whispered. "Look at me."

She looked, even as she lost herself in the mounting swell of their desire. She felt weightless, free, completely abandoned in his arms. Through a haze of sensual heat as they slowly writhed and twisted together, eyes locked, ascending to even higher plateaus of pleasure, she suddenly comprehended for the first time in her life, the meaning of "lovemaking." It was a creation they were merging to form together, a sweet, ecstatic dance of soul melding to soul.

"Love," he breathed huskily at her ear. "Love..." he repeated. And then the tenderness gave way again to a wilder burst of action. She was yielding, delighting in the submission to his urgent demands, and then it was he who was taking, eagerly responding to her passionate claims. Then it seemed not he or she but a dizzying, churning we, a fiery pinnacle of starbursts in some lofty galaxy, exploding in a savage sweetness...

Breathlessly she called his name as she fell, swooning in a warm, velvet darkness. She heard him answer as she clung to him. This passionate merging of their bodies and souls had been an exhilarating, rapturous ravishment that left her shaking beneath him, as the delirious peak of their lovemaking receded. She heard him breathe her name again. Then their breathing slowed together into a calm quiet of fulfillment.

A persistent buzzing roused her from deep, dreamless slumber. Her eyes flew open. Someone was at the door.

Amanda couldn't move. Ethan was still lying half across her on the bed. They'd never even gotten the covers down. She struggled out from under him as he softly snored, oblivious.

In the hall outside their suite was a young, uniformed hotel servant, his face barely visible over the mound of bouquets he held cradled in his arms.

"Amanda Farr?"

She nodded, disbelieving, clutching her robe closed as he walked into the room. There were a dozen bouquets of roses in all. After the boy deposited them about the sitting room, was tipped, and departed, Amanda hurried back into the bedroom. She paused at the foot of the bed. Ethan was on his back, still snoring. The sight of his beautiful nakedness brought back vivid memories of their late night passion. She couldn't resist running her hand over his muscular contours before she called his name, trying to rouse him.

"Ethan? Ethan, these flowers . . . they're gorgeous!"

"Umph?" His eyes remained shut. "Oh . . . last night . . ." he muttered, rolling over. "Ordered 'em . . . my way up . . ." He was silent then. She smiled as a gentle snore ruffled the edge of the bedsheet. She felt wide awake, but Ethan was obviously unrousable.

It took a bit of doing, but she managed to tug the covers down beneath him, and with a little prodding, got Ethan into bed. Her heart was warmed by his sleepy, childlike surrender to her ministrations. When he was tucked in comfortably, she watched him sleep for a moment. She knew then that she was totally, helplessly in love with the man.

Amanda showered. She got dressed quietly and quickly in jeans, a button-down shirt, and her pink sweater. Her stomach was beginning to growl. Ethan still couldn't be roused. A weekend of little sleep, much lovemaking, and a long night's dress rehearsal had obviously taken its toll.

Amanda took out her little datebook. She perused the addresses of the restaurants that Claudia had scribbled in there on the way to the airport. One in particular, the Cotton Café, was in Greenwich Village. Claudia had recommended it highly for breakfast. Feeling adventurous, Amanda wrote Ethan a note, telling him she'd meet him back at the hotel in the afternoon. She slipped out of the suite, leaving him to his much-needed rest.

The Village was yet another little city-within-the city. Below Fourteenth Street, there wasn't a skyscraper in sight. As the cab wended its way down narrow streets that turned this way and that, she admired the quaint, turn-of-the-century brownstones, some with little gardens or spindly trees planted in boxes along the sidewalk. The café was on Bleecker Street near Bank Street, flanked on either side by charming antique shops.

Its interior was exposed red brick and hanging ferns, and the smell of Southern-style cooking permeated the air. Amanda found a table by the window in one corner. A friendly waitress was quick with a menu and a strong cup of coffee.

She was finishing her delicious meal of eggs with onions, black-eyed peas, greens, and a hot corn muffin when she was distracted by a couple at a nearby table whose voices were raised in argument. She didn't mean to eavesdrop but the voices, too loud to ignore, sounded oddly familiar.

"I'm not blind, you know. I've watched this going on since the first rehearsal!"

"Get a grip on yourself, Jerome—you're just nervous about tonight! Your imagination's run away with you."

Amanda turned in her seat. She immediately recognized Roma, beautiful as before in an off-the-shoulder, rhinestone-studded sweatshirt. Amanda was about to turn back when Roma saw her. The actress's face immediately dropped the scowl it had worn and brightened in a smile. Roma waved her to come join them. Reluctantly, Amanda rose from her table.

"Have a seat," Roma said gaily, acting for all the world as if no altercation had been taking place. "We live right around the corner, but what brings you here? Oh, have you met Jerome?"

Amanda had enjoyed watching the tall, lanky actor on stage the day before. He was darkly handsome with the air of a moody tiger in his dark chinos and leather jacket. Now, as he held out his hand, reining in his annoyance with an effort, his sheepish smile softened his tough, streetwise manner. "Good to meet ya," he said as Amanda sat down.

"We're a little strung out this morning," smiled Roma. "Pre-opening nerves."

"Ten hours from now it'll all be over," Jerome said. "I can just see the first reviews—'Loved her, hated him.' I know it! It's gonna be brutal—a promising career finished in one night!"

"You're hysterical," said Roma. "They won't mention either of us, so don't worry."

"No mention? Great, I'll end up being a waiter the rest of my life!"

Amanda couldn't help laughing at Jerome's exaggerated nervousness. He grinned good-naturedly at her. "Cigarette? I'm on my second pack already."

"No, thanks. I'm sure you'll be great tonight," she said consolingly. "To tell you the truth, I'm a little jittery myself. This is the first Broadway opening I've ever been to, and I don't have a thing to wear."

Roma's eyes lit up. "You don't?" she exclaimed. "Let's go shopping. That's the only way to get through a day like this—buying clothes."

Jerome let out a loud groan. But despite his predictions of dire financial ruin being imminent for them both, Roma was already plotting out a tour of local boutiques. She told Amanda of a number of stores within walking distance of the café. Amanda wondered if her wariness about the young actress had been unfounded. Roma was being effusively friendly.

She called Ethan from a pay phone, hoping she wasn't waking him.

"I'm glad you called," he said, his voice still husky with sleep. "I have to go across town for an interview. I might've missed you when you came back."

"Don't you miss me now?" she joked.

"All of you," he said. "This bed is pretty cold without your warm body in it. Where are you?"

Amanda explained that she and Roma were about to go on a shopping jaunt. He was happy that she had company and some diversion while he attended to the last of his preopening chores. They agreed to meet back at the hotel toward five.

Roma whisked her in and out of the clothing stores,

both new and antique, that peppered the streets of the West Village. They soon lost Jerome, who went back to the couple's Barrow Street apartment, too nervous to deal with questions of fashion. Roma oversaw the purchase of a chic but not too expensive evening dress. She examined Amanda critically as she tried it on. The dress bared one shoulder entirely and hugged her breasts, the shimmering mauve fabric enhancing her slim hips. The material was gathered at one side so that the bottom rose diagonally, revealing more than a glimpse of leg.

"That's the one," said Roma, then squinted. "But your hair . . ."

"I've been meaning to get it cut," Amanda admitted. "But there just isn't time . . ."

"I'll be right back!" Roma hurried off to a phone. By the time Amanda was in her own clothes again, Roma was excitedly writing down the name and address of her hairstylist for her. "You're in luck," she said. "Ask for Francine. She's always open for a few hours on weekends. She's the best. She does a lot of celebrities, but she's not overpriced. She'll have a great idea for your hair, I'm sure. Can you get down there within the hour? She's had a cancellation, and she can fit you in if you hurry."

The idea of a new haircut for the opening appealed to Amanda. She wanted to look as stunning as she could for Ethan and the event. "All right," she said. "I'm game."

Francine's salon was in an unlikely loft building at the remote edge of the Lower West Side, almost by the river. Amanda had learned to expect the unexpected in Manhattan, but even so, she was unprepared for the offbeat, art-gallery space that greeted her eyes as she stepped off the creaky freight elevator.

Rock music pulsed through the wide, high-ceilinged room. Luridly colorful paintings hung on the walls, and large, kidney-shaped mirrors hung suspended above barber chairs set in the middle of the blond-wood floor. A bespectacled young man with his peroxided hair in a huge pompadour, wearing a suit from the forties, served her coffee in a waiting area inhabited by armless, bald mannequins and "new wave" jewelry displays. Next, a solemn, German-speaking fellow in a carefully paint-spattered sweatshirt washed her hair for her. Then she was hurried to a barber chair, her wet hair wrapped in a towel.

Francine herself appeared. She was a tall, svelte but brassy blonde who exuded a wisecracking worldliness Amanda found a bit intimidating. She appeared to know who Amanda was and why she was in New York. As Amanda listened to Francine chatter to her assistants, her pointed *bon mots* aimed at a number of famous names, she wondered if some underground network of cognoscenti was already abuzz with news of Ethan Taylor's latest "affair." The idea gave her shivers.

Francine darted around the chair, scissors in hand, picking up bits of Amanda's hair and letting them go with a pensive frown. "Let's go short," she announced suddenly. "Have you ever tried it?" Amanda shook her head. "Really, all of this"—she held up a handful of Amanda's hair—"is just too much. You need to free your face—look smarter, sexier!"

Amanda didn't want to be cowed by the sophisticated stylist's assured opinion. But in the mirror, her hair did look like a bedraggled mop. "Well, maybe—"

"You're used to it long," Francine noted sagely. "But I'm positive a shorter look will be an exciting change."

* * *

She was more taken aback than excited when she first beheld her "new look." Her hair was considerably shorter! No longer falling anywhere near her shoulders, it was instead cropped closely about her ears. But Amanda had to admit the new style was strikingly attractive.

Ethan was in the shower when she returned to the hotel suite. Amanda called a hello to him through the door and changed out of her clothes. She considered joining him, but couldn't resist trying on her new dress to see how it would offset her hairstyle. She had just donned the new earrings she'd purchased earlier with the dress and was stepping back to appraise her appearance in the full-length mirror on the back of the door to the bath when the door opened. Ethan stood naked in the doorway, his brawny body gleaming with beads of water as he ran a towel through his hair.

"What do you think?" she asked anxiously.

He shook the hair out of his eyes and looked at her. His eyes widened and his body stiffened. Amanda felt her blood turn to ice as he stared at her with an expression of horrified shock, the color draining from his face.

"What's wrong?" she gasped, her hands flying to her newly uncovered neck as if to shield it from his stare. "Did she cut too much? You hate it!"

Ethan quickly recovered and gave her a weak smile. "No, not at all—I just didn't recognize you for a second. I thought maybe I'd walked out of our bathroom and into someone else's suite!"

His words were almost convincing, but she sensed he'd been unnerved by something else. She rushed to the mirror, anxiously inspecting her appearance. Ethan came up slowly behind her. He bent to kiss the nape of her neck, squeezing her shoulder affectionately.

"You do hate it," she said forlornly. "I knew I shouldn't

have gone for such a radical change."

"Amanda, take it easy. I like the cut—it shows off your sexy neck—" He bent to kiss the crook of her neck again for emphasis. "It just takes a minute to get used to."

The phone rang. Ethan left her side to answer it. Amanda headed into the bathroom, still mortified despite his consoling words. Self-conscious, she stayed out of sight for quite some time, showering and remaining in the bathroom to get dressed. In between phone calls—the telephone seemed to ring every other minute now—Ethan cajoled her to come out, but Amanda stayed put.

She was putting the finishing touches on her makeup when a knock on the door to the suite announced the arrival of Casey Roberts, who was going with them to the theater. Amanda steeled herself and finally emerged. Casey greeted her appearance with an appreciative whistle.

"Hot!" was his one heartfelt word of admiration. "Hey, Ethan, where can we rent you a tux? You're about to be severely outclassed."

"Tux?" Ethan's disgruntled voice came from the other room. "This is bad enough." He entered looking more dressed up—and more ill at ease—than she had ever seen him. He looked exceptionally handsome in a three-piece, navy-blue, pin-stripe suit of worsted wool, complete with tie and cuff-linked button-down shirt. "If Broadway openings are supposedly festive, why do I feel like I'm dressed for a funeral?" Ethan winced, grappling with his tight collar. "Now I know why I never wear ties," he muttered. "They're masochistic."

Amanda laughed. "Think he'll do for an escort, Casey?"

"He'll have to, I guess." Casey winked at her, then

checked his watch. "Kristin's meeting us in the bar down-stairs. Let's hit it."

The hotel bar was a quiet, elegant, and spacious room of dark wood paneling and subdued light. Casey, even more manic than usual, insisted on buying a round for them all. His high energy served to lessen a subtle tension Amanda felt emanating from Ethan. Though he sat with his arm around her, his mind seemed to be elsewhere. He smiled at Casey's jokes, but Amanda could tell he was unusually tense.

"Is something wrong?" she whispered when Casey left them briefly to talk to an acquaintance at a nearby table.

Ethan smoothed his hair back, exhaled, and leaned against the bar. When he looked at Amanda, his eyes were affectionate, but she could read tension in his face. "I'm just preparing myself," he said quietly.

"For the critics? Or the crowd?"

He smiled. "For the whole circus." He ran the tip of his forefinger along her cheek. His gentle touch sent a delicious tremor through her body.

She put her hand over his and squeezed it. "One night in the limelight shouldn't be too hard," she kidded.

He gave her a probing look. "I wonder what this critic will have to say."

"My critical faculties don't function too well when you touch me," she told him. Ethan drew her closer and kissed her lowered eyelids.

"We'll see," he said.

"Kristin—over here!" Casey was beckoning a red-haired woman over to the bar. Amanda recognized Ethan's sister from that night at Molly's Tavern. Kristin greeted Casey with a hug and gave her brother a quick peck on the cheek. She smiled at Amanda.

"I won't say I've heard so much about you because Ethan's been typically evasive," she said when they'd been introduced. She leaned over, adding in Amanda's ear, "But he's been incredibly cheerful lately, which isn't typical at all. Glad to meet you."

Amanda smiled. She liked Kristin's lack of formality, which appeared to be a Taylor trait. As the four of them had a drink and chatted, Amanda felt the tension in the air lessen somewhat. But she caught Kristin studying her face at one point with a peculiar expression. Amanda wondered if she'd overdone her makeup.

"So," Kristin said quickly when Amanda looked at her, "what do you think of the new play?"

"I haven't seen it yet," she admitted.

Kristin turned to her brother. Again, the look in her eyes seemed strange to Amanda. "She hasn't seen it?" she asked him, sounding oddly concerned.

"She's about to," Casey announced and indicated the clock over the bar. "We should be on our way."

Blinded by the flash of a camera, Amanda pressed close to Ethan's side. Casey cleared a path for them through the swarm of first-nighters, critics, and fans. She was aware of eyes following her every move. She concentrated on following Casey's woolly mop of hair bobbing ahead and holding tight to Ethan's hand. They worked their way through the lobby, which was buzzing with conversation and opening-night electricity.

Their seats were fourth row, left of center on the aisle. Amanda felt a jolt of nervous adrenaline as she took her seat next to Ethan and started noticing faces she'd only seen before in movies and on television all around her. It seemed that everywhere she turned a celebrity was seated. The women wore their gowns and jewelry with such poise and assurance that Amanda was glad she'd gone all out for the occasion. At least she wasn't underdressed.

"It's the same production staff he used for *Dakota Angels*," someone was saying behind her. "Look at the names in the program."

"Well, with one notable exception," said his companion.

"Hmmm? Oh, yes, set design by Robin Bennett. Can't imagine he'll be as inventive as Araki was. Curious, isn't it, an Ethan Taylor play without—what, dear?"

The man's companion was whispering urgently for him to keep his voice down. As they continued talking at a lower volume, Amanda distinctly heard her own name mentioned. She couldn't help turning around for a moment. When she realized that one of the great theatrical couples of the century was talking about her, she flushed crimson and turned back in her seat. She was still clenching Ethan's hand in a viselike grip. Embarrassed, she let go and shot a glance at Ethan. He was sitting forward in his chair, gazing moodily at the curtain. She could sense his discomfort at being thrust into the public eye. He turned to look at her and gave her a knowing wink. She smiled back. Somehow, knowing he was having as hard a time relaxing made her feel less alone and vulnerable.

The lights dimmed. A rustle of anticipation coursed through the large theater. Coughs and whispers died down to an absolute stillness as the curtain rose.

On stage, soft blue lights faded up with the recorded sounds of wind and rain. The set portrayed an impoverished, ramshackle studio apartment, with the lights of a city street blinking outside a dirty window. A candle flickered on a desk by an unmade bed. The male lead was seated at the desk, writing. She leaned forward to get a better look at him in the dim light, struck by his faint resemblance to Ethan.

Ethan himself was fidgeting in his seat. No sooner had the first lines been spoken, as the actor read aloud his work-in-progress, than Ethan whispered in her ear: "I'll meet you after—next door—Casey knows where."

His lips brushed her cheek. Then he slipped quickly up the aisle. She felt abandoned momentarily but understood. The playwright was too tense to sit and watch his creation come to life. She settled back to watch the play.

On stage, a knock sounded at the door of the garret. The man rose to open it. In the doorway stood the leading lady, her oriental features framed by short black hair.

The names of the characters were different, but by the end of the first scene, Amanda was certain that she was witnessing the story of Ethan and Sono, only thinly disguised. With a mixture of dread and fascination, she hung on every line, watching their dramatic romance unfold before her. The Sono character was much as Ethan had described her, though even more admirable—a driven but noble woman, willing to sacrifice all for her struggling lover, a poet who was portrayed as gifted but ultimately selfish.

In scene after heart-rending scene, the pathos-ridden conflicts between the two were ruthlessly laid bare. Amanda found herself riveted and horrified as the woman, an artist of great stature and emotional depth, guided the young poet to prominence in his field only to have him spurn her and the very love that had nurtured him as he became successful.

Only too late, in the play's final scenes when the woman became nearly suicidal, despairing at the loss of the poet's love, were they briefly reconciled. But one felt theirs was a doomed relationship. And though the two of them were not well-matched—she, glamorously exotic and wildly emotional; he, a man of the earth with a more taciturn nature—one ultimately sympathized with the woman.

The play had much to say about the perils of pursuing fame and fortune. What it seemed to say about Ethan was devastating to Amanda. But what was especially humiliating to her was his loving portrait of his late wife, depicted in the play with open adoration.

The sound of rain that had begun the play ended it as well. Then it seemed to grow even louder as the curtain dropped, and Amanda realized she was sitting in the midst of a thunderous ovation. She herself was unable to applaud, but just sat numbly in her seat, her cheeks wet with tears. As if from a great distance, she watched the curtain calls for the leads, and then for the supporting players, including Jerome and Roma.

Judging by the applause that faded only after many more curtain calls, the play was a resounding success. Stunned, her soul in turmoil, Amanda let a jubilant Casey guide her and Kristin through the throng. She was conscious of Kristin slipping her a handkerchief, which Amanda used dazedly and returned, murmuring thanks. The lobby was a melee of enthusiastically chattering people. Casey whisked them through it, out onto the street and into a restaurant two doors down from the theater.

Ethan was at the far end of the bar. Casey gave him a thumbs-up gesture as they approached. Ethan's face brightened. He put an arm around Amanda, hugging her, as Casey pounded him on the back and Kristin beamed nearby.

"Forget about waiting for the reviews," Casey crowed.

"We have a winner. I'm surprised you couldn't hear the applause from here."

Ethan was nodding absently, not really listening, looking at Amanda with concern. "Are you all right?"

Before she could think of a suitable reply—not that she knew what to think—they were suddenly surrounded by well-wishers elbowing their way closer to Ethan. She stood quietly at his side as friends showered congratulations on the writer and director. Though Ethan held her to him protectively as people jockeyed into position to bestow their accolades, there was no way to talk. She watched Ethan grudgingly take the giddy, celebratory atmosphere in stride. Then she slipped away from him as members of the cast joined the group at the bar.

Amanda stood just beyond the tight, festive little group. She turned to the bar and froze, catching sight of her reflection in the mirror above it. She suddenly comprehended what had shocked Ethan about her appearance. Her shorter black hair was now strikingly similar to Sono's! How could she have been so unthinking? In an attempt to please him, had her own subliminal associations betrayed her or . . . ?

Roma was pushing her way closer to Ethan, her face radiant with success. As Amanda watched, the actress threw her arms around his neck and gave him a kiss full on the lips that was too long and amorous to be merely congratulatory. Jerome hovered at her side, glowering at his girlfriend with jealous resentment.

Amanda turned away, her stomach churning. Roma and her friendly advice. Francine's "suggestion." That deviously manipulating—! Humiliation seethed in her blood. She had to get out, get away, run . . .

Celebrities and sycophants still streamed in through

the door. Some looked at her curiously as she pushed her way to the exit, a lone boat against the current. Each glance was like the sting of a whip to her. Did they know? Were they mocking her, too, the silly woman trying to fill Sono Araki's shoes?

At last she gulped in the cold night air. A car horn blared as she rushed into the street, unseeing. The car that had braked to avoid hitting her was a taxi. She grabbed it.

Chapter

9

SHE HAD ONLY one bag to pack. That was the advantage, she reflected, of traveling light: She could end this affair as quickly as it had begun.

The silk negligee slowed her for a moment, and her heart gave a wrench as she pulled the bag's zipper shut. But she was determined to get out fast. Leaving a note seemed melodramatic, and what could she say? If she stopped to think at all, she might reconsider. That way lay madness. She took a last look at the lovely city view from the curtained window and walked resolutely to the door.

A key was turning in the lock. Amanda halted on the soft carpet, her heart beating loudly in her ears. Caught, she could only stand helplessly, bag in hand, as Ethan walked in the door.

He shut the door firmly behind him and stood appraising her appearance, arms folded across his chest, eyes gleaming in the semidarkness.

"In a hurry, Professor?"

"Yes." She braced herself against the warm, insinuating cadence of his husky voice.

"Where to?"

"The airport."

He frowned as he walked up to her. "Just like that? With no explanation?"

"You had a celebration to attend," she said in as cold

151

a voice as she could muster. "I didn't want to interfere."

He looked at her strangely. "You know I hate those sorts of gatherings. I was only too glad to get out of there in a hurry—but I was worried about you. Why did you leave? Why are you acting like you barely know me?"

"Because I don't know you!" she snapped.

"No?" he said, and stepped closer.

"Don't!" she said tersely, backing away. "You're only making this harder. I'm not interested in talking about things. Let's make it a clean break."

His eyes probed her angry face. "If the play upset you," he said slowly, "I think you're overreacting."

"Save the coaching for your actresses," she said bitterly. "I've got a plane to catch."

He shook his head. "You're making a mistake. I love you, Amanda."

"How can you love me? You're in love with another woman!"

He stared at her, his eyes narrowing. "You think that Roma and I—?"

"I'm sure she's just a flirtation, Ethan, much like me. I'm talking about the love of your life!"

Ethan's features set in a tight grimace of anger. "You don't know what you're talking about." His voice came out in a harsh whisper.

"I'm tired of running into Sono Araki wherever I go— up at your house, here in this city—whenever someone who knows you meets me, I'm being measured up. And then to see how you've practically deified her on stage!"

"A play isn't life, Amanda. You don't know what's based on fact and what's fabrication."

"I know enough."

She stepped around him, headed for the door. He halted her with his hand grasping her arm. "You're making a mistake," he said. "You once accused me of being too presumptuous, but now you're the one jumping to conclusions."

"I'm just facing facts," she said defiantly. "I don't know what makes you think we belong together. I don't fit into this world of yours—and I don't know if I want to! My God, I've never felt so humiliated as I did tonight. Everywhere I looked I was being judged—" She pulled her arm from his grasp. "You could have at least told me the truth when I cut my hair instead of letting me waltz right into a night of public ridicule."

"I didn't want to hurt your feelings," he said in an exasperated tone. "I wasn't sure if it was a coincidence or if you were trying to—"

"Emulate her? Give me some credit!" she stormed. "I wouldn't try; I couldn't! I'm a professor of English, damn it! I'm interested in poetry and theory, not design and fashion, and making money and whatever it is you jet-set New Yorkers fill your lives with! Honestly, Ethan, I still don't understand why you wanted to be with me to begin with!"

"Because you're you!" he exclaimed. Her pulse raced as he turned her toward him, his hands gripping her shoulders. She was forced to confront his smoldering glare. "Look at me," he said. "Don't you feel what I feel for you? Can't you trust in what we've got between us?"

Her rage made her blurt out words she instantly regretted. "Sono trusted you! And what happened to her?"

Ethan let go of her. His face was ashen, though his eyes burned like two fiery coals. "What are you saying?" he said grimly.

The fire in his eyes laced her anger with fear. She backed away, edging for the door. "Look, whatever you did in your past is your business, but it doesn't inspire great faith! The last time I trusted a man and made a commitment, I got left out in the cold. I'm not about to let it happen again."

"You're not giving me much of a chance by running out," he retorted bitterly.

"That's the idea," she snapped, picking up her bag. "I've developed survival instincts—I know when it's time to leave."

"If you weren't so hellbent on leaving, you might know more," he said. "You might know how much I need you."

Her hand was on the doorknob. She sensed the earnestness in his terse words and was swayed. But her eyes fell on the *Playbill* for Ethan's play, crumpled in the waste basket where she'd tossed it upon entering. The events of the evening came back to her in a torrent of painful images. She shuddered.

"I'm sure you can take care of yourself," she said. Before he could move to stop her, she was out the door. Bypassing the elevator, she hurried down the staircase. She sensed he might follow, but she didn't want him to. She wanted there to be no turning back.

The day dawned bleakly gray in Silver Falls. It had still been dark when she landed in Dayton, a wide-awake bundle of frayed nerves. She'd been lucky to get a flight on such short notice at that hour. But Amanda didn't feel lucky as her cab pulled out of the driveway and she mounted the staircase to her door. She felt like hell.

She dropped her bag at the foot of her bed and lay down on it fully clothed. She'd planned to rest for a minute, and then face unpacking. She sank into a dreamless sleep.

When she awoke, it was a darker gray outside. For a

moment she was completely confused. Then Amanda realized she'd slept through the day, and dusk was falling. She trundled her stiff-limbed body into the shower.

When she emerged, she felt a little better. But she was ravenously hungry. There was a can of tuna fish in her cupboard. It became dinner, one of the most depressing meals she'd ever eaten in her life. Afterward she contemplated calling Claudia for company, but the idea of reliving the whole long weekend with her friend seemed too painful. Instead, she sat in the pale blue glow of her kitchen counter light and stared at the black telephone hanging on the wall, willing it to ring. It didn't.

Amanda soon learned that walking out on Ethan Taylor had not been an effective way of removing him from her life. She walked through the next day like a zombie, unable to concentrate on her work, thankful, at least, that she didn't have classes to teach. She felt as if there were a hole in her middle, as if her very center were hollow. She ached from the loss of Ethan with an intensity beyond any emotion she'd ever felt.

Silver Falls seemed to have shrunk to pea-size in the time she was gone. The quaint homes and bucolic scenery appeared charmless to her. The campus looked as somber as a graveyard. As she walked across the brittle, frosted grass of the Main Lawn, she replayed her last scene with Ethan in her mind and felt sharp pangs of remorse. She'd been so sure she was doing the right thing. But suddenly the things they'd fought about seemed less important. In the face of this loneliness, she was ready to talk, to try to understand. If he called...

"Miss Farr!"

She looked up, startled from her reverie. Professor Hutchins, his white hair blown straight up from his forehead in the wind, was hurrying toward her, his scarf flapping around his skinny frame. He looked like a well-dressed scarecrow blown loose from his pole.

"Good afternoon, Professor."

"Yes, yes, very," he beamed, his cheeks glowing red from the cold. "I've come to congratulate you."

"Congratulate me? What for?"

"Then you haven't heard? Fine, I'll be the bearer of glad tidings, then: He's taken the residency!"

Her heart leapt. "Ethan Taylor? He's coming to Deermount?"

He squinted confusedly at her. "No, no, my dear—your Mr. McGuinness! Taylor phoned Dean Chast this morning with a refusal. The dean rang me up immediately and had me get hold of Sherman McGuinness. He's accepted!"

The hollowness in the pit of her stomach widened. She forced a weak smile as Hutchins blathered on, and she attempted to act enthused. When the old man had left her side and was scurrying off down the path, she allowed her true emotions to show. With a scowl of rage, Amanda marched across the campus.

She'd been hoping that Ethan, feeling the same loss that she felt, would be coming after her, entreating her to stay with him. But no—no sooner was she gone than he'd shut the door even more firmly behind her. She couldn't help but think that his decision was a direct result of their falling out. She'd wanted him to pursue her, open up to her. Now he'd tacitly removed any hope of reconciliation at all!

The panes of glass in her kitchen windows shook as she slammed the door behind her, storming into the apartment. The phone was ringing. She nearly yanked it off the wall in answering.

"Amanda? It's Ethan."

The sound of his husky voice made her blood boil. She was tempted to hang up. But she steeled herself, forcing a calm, level tone into her voice as she spoke.

"To what do I owe this pleasure, Mr. Taylor?"

"I've been worried about you," he said.

"I'm sure," she snapped.

"You shouldn't have run out like that."

"You didn't stop me."

"Should I have tied you to the desk?" He sighed. "Look, I'm sorry we didn't talk—about Sono—before you saw my play. I can understand your being upset."

"Good. Apology accepted. Now we can part amicably, I suppose. No hard feelings," she retorted bitterly.

"What do you mean? That's not my intention. I'm trying to talk to you, Amanda, to be honest—"

"But you haven't wasted any time in burning bridges, have you?" she interrupted.

"I don't understand."

"I just heard about the residency."

He was silent a moment. When he spoke again, she heard a cold edge in his voice. "That has nothing to do with us."

"No? I find that hard to believe."

"Why do you always assume the worst? You're finding it hard to believe me with alarming frequency." She could sense him attempting to restrain his anger. "You're just running scared, Professor."

"And you? What is it about Deermount that seems so suddenly unappealing the morning after I've left you?"

"I have another commitment," he said evenly. "I just received word that a project of mine has become solid. I'll need to be out west this summer, to see it through."

She had the sudden, awful feeling of having stepped into a recurring nightmare. "I see," she said, trying to keep the tremble out of her voice. "The Golden Boy goes Hollywood. I should have expected this."

"I am going to Los Angeles, yes—that's where the preproduction for a film of *Dakota Angels* is being done. But it's only for a month or so."

"Well, have a nice trip," she said icily. Fate was certainly being perversely unkind, punishing her like this for not having taken her experience with Brad to heart.

"Amanda, you're acting absurd!" he stormed. "First you accuse me of refusing the Deermount residency to stay away from you, and then when I explain that I have a legitimate reason, you become even more hostile!"

"I've been through this before! It's bad enough that I have to compete with Sono's memory for your love, Ethan—I'm not about to compete with the world of motion pictures!"

"You don't know what you're saying." She heard the barely controlled fury behind his words.

"I'm saying good-bye!"

She hung up quickly. Tears streamed down her cheeks as she stood, staring at nothing, feeling that the very fabric of her life had just been ripped apart. The phone rang. She disconnected it, sobbing. There was nothing to talk about. It was over.

He called the next day, but when she recognized his voice on the line, she hung up. He tried once more, and she did the same. He didn't call again after that.

Amanda sleepwalked her way through a week of classes. Each morning she would wake with a firm resolve to put Ethan in her past. Each night she'd go to bed aching with need for him. She began to wish they'd never met, wish she'd never gone to New York, wish— that he would call again...

Late in the night nearly two weeks after they had last spoken, the telephone woke her from a troubled sleep. Apprehensively, her heartbeat speeding up, she reached for the phone.

"Is this Amanda Farr?" It wasn't Ethan, but a vaguely familiar voice, rendered fuzzy by long distance static.

"Yes?"

"Amanda, it's Casey Roberts. I'm sorry to call so late. I don't mean to disturb you, but I was wondering if you possibly had heard from Ethan."

"No, not recently," she said, guarded.

"He's not there in Silver Falls?"

"Certainly not *here*," she said pointedly. "What's going on, Casey?"

"Ethan's . . . disappeared. I guess that's the word to use. He's not upstate, he's not here in the city, and we're due to meet in LA tomorrow. I thought maybe you . . ."

"Not a chance," she said. In spite of herself, she was concerned. "You sound worried, Casey."

"It's not like him to be irresponsible, that's all. I know he's been out of sorts lately, but still . . ."

"Didn't the play go over well?"

There was a pause. "Yeah," Casey said wryly. "No problems with the play." He paused again.

"Well, I hope you find him," Amanda said, affecting her breeziest tone. She wanted to hang up.

"Amanda, can I ask you one question?"

"All right."

"It's really none of my business, but the last time I did see Ethan—four days ago—he was more depressed than I'd seen him in years. What happened with you two?"

She sighed ruefully. "Nothing, Casey. I just . . . left, that's all. I'm sure he's had his share of brief affairs.

Are you trying to tell me this one was more significant than most?"

"Are we talking about the same guy?"

"What do you mean?"

"Ethan Taylor is not known for brief affairs. Look, I may be out of line here, but I've known Ethan for years, and I've never known him to get so serious so fast, as he did when he met you."

Amanda was silent. These were words she wanted to believe, but belief was difficult. "So?" she said.

"So why are you acting as if you had no effect on Ethan? I think he's in love with you. I'd say it's the first time he's been in love since..."

"He's never really gotten over her, has he?" she said, his reference to Sono stirring up her resentment again. "If you ask me, Ethan's still in her posthumous thrall."

"Is that what you think?" He sounded incredulous.

"Yes," she said, unnerved. "I saw the play on opening night, remember?"

"You saw the play," he repeated musingly. "But a play isn't real life. Maybe you should have stuck around a little longer."

Even though she sensed he was trying to be helpful, she resented his all-knowing air. "I appreciate your advice, Casey. But it's too late."

"Only if you say so."

"What do you mean?" she snapped, irritated.

"I'm sorry, Amanda. I don't mean to interfere. But if you do hear from Ethan, by some chance... Talk to him. I think there's a lot you don't know."

"I doubt I'll hear from him."

"Well, if you do... Tell him to give me a call," he finished abruptly. "Sorry to have disturbed you."

"That's all right."

"So long then, Amanda. Good luck."

When the line clicked, and she was left with the hollow whirring noises of the long-distance line in her ear, Amanda sat for a moment before she hung up, Casey's words echoing in her mind. Then she slowly replaced the receiver.

She made herself some tea in the kitchen, noting that it was well after midnight. But she was wide awake. Sleep still seemed a long ways off. It was a good thing tomorrow was Saturday.

A play isn't real life. That was what Ethan had said, too. What did it mean? What was Casey driving at? Amanda drummed her fingers on the table, then got up and paced the length of the kitchen as the water boiled. The branches of the birches rustled outside. She listened to the quiet tick of the clock on the wall. The whole building creaked in the wind as if it were a ramshackle wooden ship adrift on the sea of night.

She had a sudden, searing sensation of how utterly alone she was. She stopped in the middle of the room, staring at the table, seeing Ethan leaning against it, his eyes glowing with tender concern as he talked about taking time to get to know her. She'd believed the sincerity of his feelings for her then. Why couldn't she now?

The whistle of the kettle startled her. She turned the water off and poured her tea. She could see the moon outside the kitchen window. Clouds scurried across it as she watched. There was no keeping Ethan Taylor out of her life, she realized. Even the moon looked different to her since she'd shared it with him that magical night. She could smell the scent of hyacinth as he touched her . . .

Was it possible, As Casey had said, that Ethan felt as alone as she? Maybe she had run too soon—run scared, as Ethan had said. On the telephone, she'd barely given him a moment to explain himself. And now he was missing, deeply upset, according to one of his closest friends. Could it be that Ethan's disappearance really was the result of what she had done?

She waited for the demon voice of her wary conscience to rise up, to tell her she was a fool to believe that the man loved her. But it remained silent. The whole household seemed to hold its breath with her, silently hovering on the brink of belief, of trust.

She had a feeling she knew where Ethan might be. Her heart implored her in a wordless surge of longing to seek him out. She had to know the truth. She had to find him. Tomorrow—tomorrow, she would.

Chapter

10

THE WONDERFUL THING about a friend like Claudia was that she knew when not to ask questions. She took Amanda's request to borrow her car at nine in the morning in stride and merely cautioned her that the beat-up gray Volkswagen had no snow tires, so she had best drive carefully.

Snow had come early in the morning. When Amanda first awoke, bleary-eyed from only a few hours' restless sleep, the air outside was swirling with flakes. She'd considered postponing her mission for all of a split second, then reached for the phone to call Claudia, her determination undiminished. She bundled up in cotton tights, corduroys, a flannel shirt, wool sweater, thick socks, and her boots.

The short walk to Claudia's made her wish she'd worn a ski mask. The snow was thickening. The Volkswagen started after much coaxing and prodding, its engine cranky with the cold. "You know where you're going?" Claudia called anxiously over the motor's roar as Amanda prepared to pull out of the driveway.

"Kind of," she answered, and winced at the raised eyebrows on her friend's face. "Don't worry—I'll bring it back in one piece."

"Right—a piece of solid ice probably," said Claudia. "They're predicting a mini-blizzard on the radio."

This was disheartening news, but Amanda shrugged it off. "I'll be back as soon as I can," she called, and rolled up the window.

She had a vague idea of where Ethan's father's farm was from the things Ethan had said. She followed the same route they'd taken in his Thunderbird, heading toward Molly's Tavern. The sky was a blanket of white. She kept the windshield wipers busy as she forged ahead, driving slow. The roads were already slippery. The highway was deserted at that hour but for a lone snowplow whose masked driver peered at her inquisitively as she passed him.

She was thankful that she'd learned to drive on a stick shift and could master the clutch even though she hadn't driven such a car in the past few years. Along the way she had time to consider the confrontation ahead. What would she say to Ethan when she found him? Hello? I'm sorry? I'm ready to listen? What if he was angry? She'd face it. What if her hunch was wrong, and he wasn't at the farm? Next question...

Amanda peered through the frosting windshield. If her memory served her, Molly's would be around the bend ahead. It was. She pulled into the gravel parking lot dusted with a layer of powdery white. The lot was empty, but smoke trickled from the tavern's chimney, and the neon sign blinked brightly through the white haze.

Amanda parked, turned off the motor and hurriedly got out. The snow was already a few inches beneath her as she made her way around the building to the entrance. Thankfully, the door wasn't locked. Inside, she paused for a moment to catch her breath. Her face stung from the sudden warmth. The tavern's interior was dark, the glow of the Wurlitzer jukebox the only light besides the dim overheads at the bar. A gray-haired woman with glasses was seated at the bar on a stool, reading a newspaper and smoking a cigarette. She looked up as Amanda entered, then returned to her paper.

Amanda walked across the sawdust floor and hovered at the older woman's side, uncertain of what tack to take. "Is this place open? For business, I mean."

The woman regarded her silently over her glasses, then nodded. "You won't find breakfast here, though," she said in a raspy, gravel-toned voice. "And it's a bit early for drinking, don't you think?"

The woman's wry, assured manner indicated she wasn't a customer. Amanda intuited that she was the owner. "Are you Molly?" she asked.

The woman nodded again and stubbed out her cigarette in a nearby ashtray. "What can I do for you? Coffee?"

"Actually, I need some directions," Amanda said. She slipped onto the stool next to Molly. "I'm trying to find the Taylor farm."

Molly lifted her chin and peered at Amanda through her glasses. Their thickness gave her an owlish look. "The Taylor farm?" she repeated.

"I understand that Mr. Taylor lives not far from here. His son comes in here a lot. I . . ." Amanda was embarrassed by the woman's piercing stare, but she plunged on. "I was here with him one night not long ago, and the people here seemed to know him, so I thought . . ." Her words trailed off lamely. She pursed her lips as the woman continued staring at her. "Do you know the Taylors?"

Molly ignored her last question, intent on taking out a pack of cigarette papers and a tobacco pouch from her denim shirt pocket. "You from the university?" she asked, spilling some tobacco onto the paper in her gnarled hand.

"Yes, I teach at Deermount. That's where I—"

"Don't know as I can help you," Molly said, swiftly rolling up the cigarette one-handed. "Sorry."

Amanda watched her pop the cigarette into her mouth and light it. She felt helpless before the woman's implacable air, and especially frustrated because she could sense that Molly knew more than she was telling. Amanda remembered the waitress in New York, and the way people who knew Ethan had of protecting him from the public.

"Look," she said. "I'm not going to say this is an emergency because it isn't. But I wouldn't be driving around in a snowstorm looking for Ethan Taylor if it wasn't important. I'm not a reporter, or a fan, or a pest— I'm not family either, but I . . ." Molly was looking at her with a gleam of amused curiosity in her eyes. "I need to find him, damn it! And I think he needs me to find him. So if by any chance you do know how I could do that, even if he doesn't like people trying to track him down, he—I think he'd appreciate it," she finished abruptly, feeling her cheeks redden.

Molly exhaled a smoke ring and watched it float in the air. Amanda felt she'd said all she could say without making a complete fool of herself. She sighed and got up from the stool. She couldn't wring the information she needed out of this woman. Maybe there was a gas station down the road where she'd have better luck. Muttering a thanks, she turned to leave.

"You know your way back?" Molly said suddenly. Amanda nodded. "Well, there's two ways, actually," the woman drawled, and puffed on her cigarette. "If you continue down Route 90, for example, there's a turn-

off. A kind of scenic route." She looked over her glasses
at Amanda with a meaningful squint.

"Yes," Amanda said, her heartbeat quickening. "And
then?"

Molly exhaled a series of little rings. "Well, if one
were to take that turn-off—it's a left on Harrison Road—
follow it to Indian Hill Drive, and take a right..." She
paused to tap her ash. "You'd pass a lot of nice farm
country on that drive. One, two, oh, maybe three nice
parcels of land over the hill there." She looked at Amanda
again, poker-faced. "Might be tough goin' if this snow
keeps up. You'd probably want to just follow 90 on back
to Silver Falls."

Amanda nodded, her mind busily memorizing: a left,
a right, three farms down. "Thank you," she said with
a grateful smile.

'You're welcome," Molly said gruffly, and picked up
her newspaper. "If he has a fit, it'll be on your pretty
little head, not mine," she muttered. "Drive careful."

Amanda stifled her impulse to hug the very neck she'd
wanted to wring moments ago and called another thanks
to Molly as she hurried to the door. Emerging, she was
blinded. Snow flew in her eyes. The wind had picked
up and howled in her ears.

The little Volkswagen resisted her efforts on the first
two tries, but grudgingly kicked into activity on the third.
Amanda steered her way carefully down the highway's
slick surface. She was driving through a world of white.
The car's frame shook in the gusts of wind. She nearly
missed the turn-off onto Harrison Road, and when she
braked, the wheels spun crazily for a terrifying moment.
She gained control of the car and eased it back in the
right direction.

Harrison Road was winding and hilly. She began to

feel she was on some perverse obstacle course. She had
to grip the wheel with both hands and stay in second
gear, straining to see the road in front of her. As the trip
appeared unending, she began to fantasize that Molly
had intended to send her off on a wild goose chase.
Swearing under her breath at each new turn, rise, and
dip in the road, Amanda felt all her muscles tighten with
anxiety as she craned her neck, her face only inches from
the windshield.

A signpost loomed in front of her. It was lopsided
and snow-covered, but an "ill" that indicated "Hill" was
legible, so she gambled it was the right one. Even as she
breathed a sigh of relief, turning off the road with pains-
taking caution, her stomach plummeted. There was barely
a road to drive on as far as she could see. It seemed that
an unbroken expanse of white lay ahead of her. Only by
opening her window and staring at the scenery could she
discern the subtle outlines of an obviously rarely traveled
road. The wind blew small clouds of snow in her face
as she leaned out the window, steering as best she could
down the narrow, winding drive.

Then disaster struck. Her foot pressed the pedal, but
the car didn't move. The wheels were spinning in place,
showering the sides of the car with snow. She wanted
to scream with the tires in frustration. Judging by the
skewed tilt of the car, she'd driven into a ditch. She tried
reverse. The car slid back a foot, then stopped with a
jolt. Now the rear wheels drove a shower of snow up.
First gear yielded no movement at all. The car was stuck.

Amanda swore, invoked the gods, and counted to
twenty, the motor idling. Then she attempted to maneuver her way out once more. All that she got for her efforts
was a faceful of snow from the spinning wheels.

She pounded the steering wheel and shut off the engine. She didn't have much choice. She could sit in the damned ditch and let the gathering snow turn her car into a tomb, or she could get out and walk. She wrenched the door open and got out. Her boots sank into a drift. Mini-blizzard, indeed.

Amanda wrapped her scarf around her mouth and ears. She could tell where the road lay by the position of the trees that lined it. She took a deep breath and began to trudge down the road. A few times she had to stop in her tracks and wait for the wailing wind to subside. The icy flakes bombarded her face.

Soon she glimpsed the first of the three farmhouses, a vague dark shape in the whiteness beyond a ridge of naked, shaking elms. But no sooner was she past it than it seemed to Amanda that she was in a desert of freezing white. She couldn't distinguish any shapes on either side of her. She fervently prayed that her sense of direction was accurate. If she was wandering off the road and into acres of farmland, she'd never know it.

Her ears burned with the cold. Her eyelashes were frozen. Her eyes were in a constant blink, and her hands in her woolen mittens felt like icicles. You and your big ideas, she told herself. You could have tracked him down by phone.

She stumbled against something, lost her balance, and fell back into the frigid wet drifts. Picking herself up with a groan, she realized she'd walked into a wooden fence. Squinting against the blinding whirls of snowfall, she could make out the line of posts stretching ahead into the white mist. At least if she followed the fence, she had a navigational guide. She began to walk alongside it. Now and then she had to hold onto the wooden slats as the wind threatened to whip her off her feet.

Still there was nothing she could see besides the fence. For all she knew the next farm was a mile away, maybe two. That was a horrifying thought. Her legs were already weary with the effort of withstanding the wind and trudging through the snow. Her pants were soaked. Onward, she commanded her feet even as a spray of icy flakes blinded her again, and she doubled over against the sudden raging assault of frigid wind.

She didn't hear the motor until the car was almost upon her. She stood transfixed, her heart leaping as the car door slammed and a tall, dark figure rose like a vision before her.

"Amanda!"

She gasped, her lips too cold to form his name in answer. But her hands flew up to reach for him as she stumbled forward, her blood surged with joy as she swooned into Ethan Taylor's arms. All her prepared apologies and accusations melted away in the delicious warmth of his embrace.

The snow swirled around them and the wind still howled, but all she felt was the powerful heat of his body against hers; all she heard was his husky murmuring of her name as he kissed her frozen ears, cheeks, lips. She let him half-lead, half-carry her to the pickup truck. She clung to him, radiantly grateful for his protection, as he flung the door open and hustled her inside.

Then he was in the truck beside her, cupping her chin in his warm hand and bending to kiss her frozen lips, quieting the chatter of her teeth. His arm encircled her back as he pulled her even closer. "You little fool," he murmured. "It's a good thing Molly had second thoughts about sending a stranger out to Dad's farm in this storm and gave me a call. You could have been—"

"I'm here," she interrupted. "That's all that matters, isn't it?"

He gazed at her, smiling. "You're right, Professor. I've missed you more than words..." His lips finished the sentence, seeking hers with a breathtaking desire. Their kiss was long. He savored all the sweetness of her mouth as she reexplored his. Their tongues circled, sending tremors of excitement through her.

When at last they broke apart, he looked at her adoringly, searching out the details of her face just as she eagerly drank in the sight of his. He kissed her once more briefly, then turned his attention to the road. "I'm taking you home," he said, turning the steering wheel.

The truck was better equipped to handle the road, and Ethan knew his way. Amanda watched in silence as he turned them around and headed down the road she'd been traversing on foot. She leaned against him, reveling in the nearness of him. He hugged her to him, one arm still around her as he drove. He kept shaking his head as if in disbelief at her arrival. She kissed his neck, suddenly unable to stop smiling.

"Are you thawing out?" he asked.

"Slowly."

"I just built a fire at the farm." He looked at her quickly, then turned his eyes back to the road. The images stirred up in her by his words made her skin tingle. She forced herself to remember the reason she'd braved this storm in the first place.

"Ethan, I have some questions to ask you—questions that I guess I should have asked sooner."

He nodded. "Ask now."

Amanda let out a deep breath. "You said your mourning was over...but I've felt you're still in love with Sono. If your play didn't really tell the story of how it was between the two of you, then what *did* happen? I need to know the truth, Ethan."

They were pulling up the driveway of a looming gray farmhouse. Ethan turned off the ignition. The motor died. All was silent but for the muffled howling of the wind outside.

"I did love Sono Araki, once," he said slowly. "But my love died long before she did." He looked at Amanda. "By the time Sono died, we were barely speaking. In a way, I hated her."

"But then . . . those rumors—"

"That I drove her to it?" He sighed. "Hardly. Maybe if I had known of her intentions, I could have tried to stop her. I owed her that much. That's exactly the thought that haunted me for so long . . ." He shook his head. "Come inside with me. I'll start from the beginning."

The trip from the truck to the house was a blur of icy white. She let Ethan hustle her up to the door and inside, her mind a dazed whir of half-formed thoughts and questions. In moments they were standing before a crackling stone hearth. Ethan took her mittens from her and put them on the warm stones. She spread her numb hands over the fire. "But you worked together for years . . ." she murmured, confused.

"Worked, yes. We had a very successful professional relationship. It was the marriage that was a mistake." He helped Amanda out of her coat, then drew a stool up by the fire for her to sit on. When she was settled, Ethan leaned against the stone mantel and pushed his hair back, staring into the flames.

"When I met Sono Araki, I was nobody and she was someone," he began. "I was in awe of her and very impressionable. She came into the Dugout Theater one night when we were doing my first one-act play. Stayed after the show and struck up a conversation. She ripped down this tacky set we had, with her bare hands, hung up one sheet and stuck a coatrack here, a chair there, changed some lighting set-ups, and it looked like a million dollars. My awe turned into infatuation. We went out for a drink. I guess you could say we just kept going, from that night on."

He paused and cleared his throat. "I was young and inexperienced in those days. I'd never had a woman lavish so much attention on me. She believed in my work at a time when most people thought I should give it up. She introduced me to the right people and showed me how to do the right things . . . I'd never known anyone like her. I didn't understand her, but she fascinated me." He paused again, glanced at Amanda, then looked away. "I hate to admit it," he went on in a subdued voice, "but I do believe that when we first became lovers, I was trying in some misguided way to repay the kindness she'd shown me." He shook his head. "It was a major mistake. I wasn't that serious, but she certainly was. I didn't realize the price I'd really have to pay, not then. Sono wanted more than a protégé or a lover. She wanted to own me, body and soul."

He looked back at Amanda. She could see the sadness in his eyes as he went on quietly: "By then, we were working together. We had our first mutual success. It was pretty heady stuff for me. We were still getting along at the time, so when she told me she was pregnant . . . I did the proper thing—that is, what I thought was proper. We got married in the midst of our most ambitious production. A few months later, she miscarried—supposedly. It wasn't until years later that I found out there never had been any baby."

"You mean she lied?"

He nodded. "I was showing some signs of straying. I was beginning to know her better, and I wasn't too comfortable with the Sono I was coming to know. She sensed it, so . . . I guess you could call it emotional black-mail." He sighed. "Remember when you told me about how Brad and you lived together but had grown further and further apart? That was the story with Sono and me, in spades. Our marriage was a kind of charade."

"Then why didn't you—?"

"Sono wouldn't hear of a divorce, no way!" He bent over to stoke the fire briefly, then leaned against the mantel, facing her. "That woman had a ton of pride. She'd snagged herself a reputed genius, which is what she'd always wanted, I suppose. And the damnable thing is, when we were in a theater, we made a great team, brought out the best in each other. It was at home that we brought out the worst." He looked into the fire again, shadows flickering over his profile. "Even when it was obvious that whatever affection there had been between us was long gone, she still tried to run my life. She tried to call the shots when I was in a position to call my own. When I resisted . . ." He took a deep breath, then exhaled slowly. "Hell had no fury, as they say. Only Sono took it out on everyone else. She became impossible to work with. It's ironic, but after a while I was about the only one in theater circles willing to take her on."

A log shifted and sputtered. Amanda stared at the fire, then looked up to meet Ethan's eyes. "But in your play, you made her seem so attractive—your relationship with her, so romantic—and your character was the one who appeared to be most at fault."

"Sono had threatened suicide before—as I became more distant from her—but I never took her seriously. When she died, of course I blamed myself. I hadn't tried to prevent it, I'd made her unhappy, I hadn't loved her as I should have. They say the survivor always feels guilty when a loved one, a family member dies. In my case the guilt was a little more plausible, a little more tangible than most . . .

"I wrote that play," he continued, his voice low and fraught with pain, "to purge my conscience."

"I'm not sure I understand."

"By the time Sono died, she was far from well-liked. She hadn't gotten what she claimed she wanted—my love—so she threw herself into her work with vengeance. Her cruelty to other theater people became legendary. After she was gone, I tried to recapture what had been beautiful about her, before the ugliness inside her overshadowed it. Sure, I romanticized her character in my play. I did it on purpose—I owed her, Amanda. I was only trying to rub the tarnish off her reputation. It was the least—the very least—I could do."

Amanda nodded thoughtfully. "I see."

"Do you?"

He left the mantel to kneel beside her, his velvet eyes caressing her face with a searching gaze. "Can you accept the fact that I love you for being you, that your differences from Sono are the things I love about you the most? *You're* everything I've ever wanted in a woman. I've been trying to tell you that all along. I wish you'd believe me."

"I want to," she murmured.

Ethan drew her to him. He kissed a line of warm kisses down her cheek, then found her mouth and ruthlessly plundered the pliant softness of her lips.

"I want . . ." she breathed as she felt the surge of fiery passion spark and soar between them.

When they broke from a kiss that reawakened all of

her desire, Ethan's voice was husky with arousal. "You should get out of those wet clothes," he said.

They rose together from the fireplace. Ethan showed her to a little bathroom off the living room of the farmhouse and provided her with a towel.

"Ethan?"

Amanda opened the bathroom door a few inches and leaned out. She'd hung her wet clothes up on the shower rod and now, clad only in the towel, was in a quandary over her next move. Ethan sauntered into view, his maroon chamois shirt unbuttoned over his tight jeans. "Yes?"

"I can't wander around here half-naked, Ethan. What if your father—?"

"He's still fast asleep upstairs," he answered, smiling. "But if you'd feel more at ease, try on my robe. It's hanging on the back of the door."

Ethan's bathrobe was a worn but comfortable flannel, and many sizes too large. Amanda belted it tight around her waist and joined Ethan by the fire in the large, homey living room. She sat by him on the rug, modestly covering her legs, and took the large mug of hot coffee he held out to her. She took a sip, then set it down and leaned into Ethan's waiting arms, luxuriating in the feel of his muscular body against hers. She looked up to see the firelight dancing in his eyes.

"I'm sorry I ran away," she said. "I should have listened to you when you tried to explain..."

"And I should have explained myself sooner," he said, pulling her closer to him. "I guess my own trust mechanism had grown a bit rusty." He leaned over to kiss the soft skin at the nape of her neck, and a delicious tremor shook her at his touch. "Now that you're here," he said softly, "I'm not letting you run away again."

"How do I know, though," she asked, sitting up, "that

you won't be the one to run? You're going to Hollywood this summer. You'll have one project or another coming up right after that, I'm sure. And you live over six-hundred miles away!"

"You're right," he said. "It's a difficult situation. That's why it would be a lot easier if you married me."

She turned to stare at him, her mouth dropping open. "You've got a strange sense of humor," she managed, her heart beating wildly.

He raised his eyebrows. "Who's joking? I think we should do it this spring, maybe in April... What's wrong?"

Amanda had scrambled to her feet and was standing with her back to the roaring flames, an equally turbulent fire in her eyes. "Of all your assumptions, Ethan Taylor, this one is the most—the most outrageous! What on earth makes you think I'd marry you?"

"Well, we love each other," he said. "That is, I know I love you. Isn't that clear to you by now? And I do believe that you love me."

"That may be so," she said, exasperated. "Though how I could love a man as arrogant as you are is a mystery. But what are you thinking of? If you think I'm going to give up my career and move to New York just like that, you're not only presumptuous, you're crazy!"

"Hold on, Professor," he said mildly. "I'm not asking you to move. I'm the one who's moving—here, to Ohio."

"What? Since when? Why didn't you tell me?"

"I had my plans made when I decided not to take that summer residency. As I told the dean, I might easily be available at a later time.... Didn't he tell you? Anyway, Amanda, it's why I called you, but you wouldn't let me tell you anything." He frowned. "You were too busy reacting to the Brad-alarms you heard going off behind everything I said. As it is, I've bought the farm that adjoins this one. I looked it over on my last trip when I saw that it was up for sale. Now I can be close to my Dad *and* a certain college in a neighboring town." He chuckled as she continued to stare at him. "Do you mind?"

Amanda shook her head. "But your cottage in New York—"

"I've been wanting to get out of that place for some time now. I've had ghosts of my own to exorcize. And finding you has clinched it for me."

Amanda walked to the mantelpiece and leaned against it, looking at Ethan. "Ethan, part of me loves you dearly for feeling that way. And part of me . . . well—"

"Well what? Why are you so reluctant?"

"Ethan, I'm an English professor. Even if I could adjust to dealing with theater people again—I'm not a cosmopolitan woman. Hardly. New York City and your high-society friends intimidated me if you want to know the truth. And the very thought of setting foot in Hollywood gives me the creeps. I don't know how to be fashionable—I don't take well to extravagance—and I'd hate being monitored by gossip columns. It's all an alien world to me. I don't fit in it."

"Neither do I," he said simply. "Come here. Amanda— please." He held his hand out. Sighing, Amanda moved from the fireplace and sank to her knees at Ethan's side. He gazed at her as he took her hand in his and squeezed it gently. "Remember me?" he asked. "I'm the guy who equates a tuxedo with a straitjacket. I don't come from that—high society, as you call it—I'm the original misfit there. I've learned how to move in those circles, sure, but I don't hang out in them. When I was younger, I thought I had to. Now I know I don't. Once a year there's an opening night perhaps . . . but the rest of the time I do what I like. I like to write. I like the woods, the countryside. And the money I make goes into things that matter—like building a new home. I'd like to build one with you."

Amanda looked down at her hand in his, feeling the warm pulse of their blood. She was silent. Ethan slid his arm around her and caressed her back.

"Well?"

She shook her head. His touch was sending little tremors of arousal through her. "It's just..."

"Just what? What else is there that makes the idea of marriage to me seem so troublesome?"

"Because you left something out!" she said. "Something important. You didn't really *ask* me—and I haven't said yes."

"Ah," said Ethan. He looked at her, a smile lighting up his face. "I didn't mean to skip that part, my love." He drew her to him, sitting up to face her. "Will you marry me?"

She looked into his eyes and saw the love there. Then she looked away, feeling a happiness that surpassed joy coursing through her in a sudden wave. The beginnings of a smile danced at the corners of her mouth. "I'll have to think about it," she told him.

His eyes widened. "You won't say yes?"

"No."

He stared at her a moment, then smiled as well. "I'll have to persuade you then." He kissed her. His lips moved to her eyelids and temples, then to her sensitive neck, his tongue enticingly encircling one earlobe as he guided her gently downward with him to the thick rug. A moan escaped her as he pressed his mouth to the hollow at the base of her neck.

"Say yes," he whispered.

She shook her head, her only answer a shuddering

sigh of pleasure. Ethan's hand was deftly loosening the belt of her robe. She gasped as his soft, firm fingers gently stroked her trembling flesh. She tangled her fingers in his damp hair, their tongues spiraling once more, her blood pounding as his caresses became more urgent.

Soon she was fumbling with him at his buttons and zipper, eager to feel his lithe nakedness against hers. His lips played over her breasts, teasing and tantalizing her. "Say yes," he breathed again.

She closed her eyes, giving a little groan of demurral. But when his hand slipped between her knees, stroking and tickling its way higher, she became breathless with desire for him. She wrapped her arms around him, pulling him down to her. Still he paused, hovering on the brink of satisfying her aching need. She opened her eyes to see his smiling face above hers. She squirmed and thrust herself to welcome him, his continual caresses by now an agony of arousal to her. He held himself back, looking at her expectantly.

"Damn you," she breathed. "Yes!" At last he lowered himself, and all reason fled her mind as they were joined, ecstasy flooding her as she surrendered to her deep love for him. For a long moment they merely held each other, still, content to revel in this exquisite, long-awaited union.

"Promise me one thing," he whispered.

"What thing?" she managed weakly.

"Promise me you'll let your hair grow."

Amanda smiled. "No problem," she said.

"Amanda," he whispered, smiling, and claimed her mouth with a kiss as sweet as dreams come true.

Second Chance at Love ®

____ 07239-7 **MOONLIGHT ON THE BAY #151** Maggie Peck
____ 07240-0 **ONCE MORE WITH FEELING #152** Melinda Harris
____ 07241-9 **INTIMATE SCOUNDRELS #153** Cathy Thacker
____ 07242-7 **STRANGER IN PARADISE #154** Laurel Blake
____ 07243-5 **KISSED BY MAGIC #155** Kay Robbins
____ 07244-3 **LOVESTRUCK #156** Margot Leslie
____ 07245-1 **DEEP IN THE HEART #157** Lynn Lawrence
____ 07246-X **SEASON OF MARRIAGE #158** Diane Crawford
____ 07247-8 **THE LOVING TOUCH #159** Aimée Duvall
____ 07575-2 **TENDER TRAP #160** Charlotte Hines
____ 07576-0 **EARTHLY SPLENDOR #161** Sharon Francis
____ 07577-9 **MIDSUMMER MAGIC #162** Kate Nevins
____ 07578-7 **SWEET BLISS #163** Daisy Logan
____ 07579-5 **TEMPEST IN EDEN #164** Sandra Brown
____ 07580-9 **STARRY EYED #165** Maureen Norris
____ 07581-7 **NO GENTLE POSSESSION #166** Ann Cristy
____ 07582-5 **KISSES FROM HEAVEN #167** Jeanne Grant
____ 07583-3 **BEGUILED #168** Linda Barlow
____ 07584-1 **SILVER ENCHANTMENT #169** Jane Ireland
____ 07585-X **REFUGE IN HIS ARMS #170** Jasmine Craig
____ 07586-8 **SHINING PROMISE #171** Marianne Cole
____ 07587-6 **WRAPPED IN RAINBOWS #172** Susanna Collins
____ 07588-4 **CUPID'S REVENGE #173** Cally Hughes
____ 07589-2 **TRIAL BY DESIRE #174** Elissa Curry
____ 07590-6 **DAZZLED #175** Jenny Bates
____ 07591-4 **CRAZY IN LOVE #176** Mary Haskell
____ 07592-2 **SPARRING PARTNERS #177** Lauren Fox
____ 07593-0 **WINTER WILDFIRE #178** Elissa Curry
____ 07594-9 **AFTER THE RAIN #179** Aimée Duvall
____ 07595-7 **RECKLESS DESIRE #180** Nicola Andrews
____ 07596-5 **THE RUSHING TIDE #181** Laura Eaton
____ 07597-3 **SWEET TRESPASS #182** Diana Mars
____ 07598-1 **TORRID NIGHTS #183** Beth Brookes
____ 07800-X **WINTERGREEN #184** Jeanne Grant
____ 07801-8 **NO EASY SURRENDER #185** Jan Mathews
____ 07802-6 **IRRESISTIBLE YOU #186** Claudia Bishop
____ 07803-4 **SURPRISED BY LOVE #187** Jasmine Craig
____ 07804-2 **FLIGHTS OF FANCY #188** Linda Barlow
____ 07805-0 **STARFIRE #189** Lee Williams

All of the above titles are $1.95
Prices may be slightly higher in Canada.

HERE'S WHAT READERS ARE SAYING ABOUT

Second Chance at Love ®
™

"I think your books are great. I love to read them as does my family."
— *P. S., Milford, MA**

"Your books are some of the best romances I've read."
— *M. B., Zeeland, MI**

"SECOND CHANCE AT LOVE is my favorite line of romance novels."
— *L. B., Springfield, VA**

"I think SECOND CHANCE AT LOVE books are terrific. I married my 'Second Chance' over 15 years ago. I truly believe love is lovelier the second time around!"
— *P. P., Houston, TX**

"I enjoy your books tremendously."
— *I. S., Bayonne, NJ**

"I love your books and read them all the time. Keep them coming—they're just great."
— *G. L., Brookfield, CT**

"SECOND CHANCE AT LOVE books are definitely the best!"
— *D. P., Wabash, IN**

*Name and address available upon request